C EY

"FIND THEM, N3."

"Find out why that CIA man was killed and who attacked you. The murdered CIA man was Paul Lyons. His cover was on the staff in the Paris main office of Carr et Frères, a French food company that does a lot of business in Africa and was involved in aid efforts. Your cover will be that you're CIA."

"Cover or bait," Carter said.

"You knew the job was dangerous when you took it, N3." Hawk's voice became a distant chuckle.

NICK CARTER IS IT!

"Nick Carter out-Bonds James Bond."
—*Buffalo Evening News*

"Nick Carter is America's #1 espionage agent."
—*Variety*

"Nick Carter is razor-sharp suspense."
—*King Features*

"Nick Carter has attracted an army of addicted readers . . . the books are fast, have plenty of action and just the right degree of sex . . . Nick Carter is the American James Bond, suave, sophisticated, a killer with both the ladies and the enemy."

—*New York Times*

FROM THE NICK CARTER
KILLMASTER SERIES

NICK CARTER

KILLMASTER

Mercenary Mountain

C

CHARTER BOOKS, NEW YORK

MERCENARY MOUNTAIN

A Charter Book/published by arrangement with
The Condé Nast Publications, Inc.

PRINTING HISTORY
Charter edition/March 1986

ISBN: 0-441-52510-5

Charter Books are published by The Berkley Publishing Group,
200 Madison Avenue, New York, New York 10016.
PRINTED IN THE UNITED STATES OF AMERICA

*Dedicated to the men of the
Secret Services of the
United States of America*

ONE

Clouds of dust rose from the steep dirt road scorched by the long, rainless years of African sun in the Eritrean back country of northeastern Ethiopia. The heat baked into the rock, the rock pounded to dust by hundreds of thousands of bare, skeletal feet as the starving natives of Eritrea left their dead farms to struggle toward the last hope of food in the refugee camps set up by the international aid committees.

The endless column of white-clad victims of Africa's longest drought in recent memory stretched almost out of sight in both directions, a column that moved slowly, with many gaps, as the weakened victims of years of hunger stumbled and shuffled ahead, their ranks thinning with each moment. Some collapsed on the road with their bloated bellies and protruding bones, others staggered off to sprawl into the ditches and thorny underbrush, too exhausted to move farther.

Through this ragged column of despair a fast-moving patrol of the Ethiopian army pushed its way. The soldiers shoved and kicked the starving refugees out of their path, laughing as they pushed some particularly emaciated man who staggered to fall facedown into the dust. The stronger of the ragged horde moved to get out of the path of the well-fed soldiers, but most only stumbled on, oblivious to anything beyond their hunger, and the weakest collapsed at the touch of the soldiers to lie unmoving wherever they fell. The soldiers barely glanced at the near dead walkers. These were, after all, Eritreans. Rebels. The enemy. Let them starve.

At a spot where the mountains towered close to the dusty road that descended toward the plain and the aid camps, the officer in charge of the patrol made a sharp motion with his arm. The soldiers turned and left the road on a narrow trail that wound up the steep slope into the brush and tinder-dry trees. They vanished in seconds, and the stream of miserable humanity flowed on as if the soldiers had never been there. For most of them, sunk in pain and hunger and weakness, the soldiers never had.

One tall man, his tattered rags flapping over his black skin, his turban so filthy it was impossible to believe it had ever been white, his skin so dusty it was more gray than black, staggered after the vanished patrol, drawn like a moth to the sound of their passage, pulled inexorably by their very speed, their power. An animal following anything that moved in the hope of food.

The rear soldier of the patrol glanced back at the road and the river of refugees and saw the ragged peasant weaving and struggling after them, his eyes rolled up to the sky as if blind, his mouth open and gasping for air. The soldier dropped back and kicked the refugee's feet out from under him. The ragged man crashed down into the dust and brush and lay motionless.

"Eat dirt, pig," the soldier muttered. "It will teach

you not to defy your leaders."

The soldier hurried back to his post at the rear of the patrol. The column vanished on through the brush. Silence descended on the mountainside. There was only the shuffle of feet down on the barren road, and the cries of birds in the dry trees.

The peasant raised his head. The eyes that had been turned blindly up to the sky quickly surveyed the hidden hillside. He was alone. He leaped to his feet, moved off the trail, and ran forward in a silent, ground-covering stride parallel to the path. He seemed to glide like a snake through the thick brush, as silent as a ghost, and as unseen.

He caught up with the hurrying patrol down on the path and then settled into an effortless, long-striding walk parallel to the soldiers. Together they moved on up the mountainside, the soldiers single-file on the narrow trail, the ragged, unseen peasant twenty yards up the side of the mountain among the thick brush and trees.

A mile in from the road the officer raised his hand in a small clearing on the mountainside. The patrol came to a sharp halt. The officer looked, listened, and then signaled his men to take up positions around the perimeter of the small clearing. The officer sat down with his back against a thick tree, lit a long Russian cigarette, and blew lazy streams of smoke. He seemed to be waiting, was in no hurry, enjoying his ease and his cigarette.

Up on the side of the mountain the still unseen peasant in the ragged turban watched.

The sharp call of a bird came from somewhere ahead along the trail.

The officer in the clearing sat up, his cigarette held motionless.

On the mountain the hidden peasant listened.

The call of the bird came again. It was a good imitation, but to the ears of the peasant, not quite good enough. The officer in the clearing waited for a third call. Then he cupped his hands and gave a return call.

The officer stood, motioning orders to his men. They spread out through the trees to cover the clearing. The officer watched the trail ahead. His slender black hand rested on the butt of his pistol.

On the mountainside the peasant aimed a powerful pair of binoculars at the pair. They came into focus as they were greeted by the patrol officer. He could see that one was an Ethiopian general, and the second a short, stocky civilian wearing a khaki bush jacket with the symbol of a U.N. observer on its breast pocket.

He moved the binoculars to observe the civilian's right hand with its four rings. The stocky man's left hand was missing the tip of the third finger. Then he studied the tall, erect general with his smart khaki uniform and Sam Browne belt despite the heat and the rugged country. He returned the binoculars to their pocket in his filthy turban and withdrew a small, rectangular case from under his ragged robes.

As the general, the civilian, and the patrol officer conferred in the center of the clearing under the guns of the alert soldiers of the patrol, the hidden watcher on the mountainside opened the case and assembled a short, compact rifle with a telescopic sight. Prone, he aimed at the conference in the clearing below.

"Ahhhhnnnnnnnhhnnnnnnnnnnnnn!"

The scream of agony shattered the forest. A cloud of birds rose into the air from the dry trees. Animals scurried through the thick brush. In the clearing the soldiers stared along the trail from where the general and the civilian had come.

"Nnnnnnhhhhhhh . . ."

The groan of pain strangled into silence at the edge of the clearing where two soldiers appeared dragging something torn and red and bleeding. Its face was a mass of purplish-black bruises and blood, its clothing so ripped and bloody it was almost unrecognizable as clothing, the thing itself almost unrecognizable as a man. But it was a man, beaten and tortured into something no longer human.

The general's voice carried across the distance.

"Well?"

One of the soldiers dragging the nearly unconscious man answered.

"He would say nothing more, General."

"Oh? Then why do we need him?"

The tall general, immaculate in his starched uniform and Sam Browne belt, drew his pistol, posed for a moment with the barrel against the unconscious man's bloody head, and fired. The two soldiers let the body fall into the forest dirt.

On the mountainside the hidden man fired his compact rifle in the echo of the execution.

In the clearing the civilian in the bush jacket with the U.N. emblem was hurled backward and fell heavily, his arms flung out, his eyes staring up at the thick mass of branches of the forest roof, blood soaking into the dirt around his head.

"Up there!" the patrol officer shouted.

The soldiers rushed toward the rise of the mountain. The ragged man picked off two before they had taken three steps, bloody brain matter and bone fragments splattering over those behind them. The others dived for cover. The general fell behind a tree.

"Get me out of here!" he bawled.

The patrol officer turned. "But, General, up there—"

"The hell with whoever's up there! Get your men around me and get me away from here now!"

The younger officer barked commands. The soldiers half scurried, half crawled backward away from the slope of the mountain to where the general waited behind his tree. The young Ethiopian officer looked back to where the hidden peasant watched. Disgust written all over him, he motioned to his men. With the general cowering in the middle of them, they marched back down the trail toward the distant road and the endless stream of refugees.

There was silence in the forest.

Even the birds were gone.

The tall man on the slope stood up in his filthy turban and tattered native clothing. He listened for some time. There was no sound. Nothing moved. Down in the dusty clearing the four bodies lay with their blood still spreading around them. Slowly the birds began to call, sing, cry to each other high in the trees. Animals moved warily in the brush. The man with the sniper rifle walked down the mountainside to the clearing.

He stood for a time looking off in the direction where the patrol and the general had vanished. He laughed out loud.

"That's one general who values his own skin," he said to the trees and brush and now singing birds.

Then he bent to examine the two dead civilians. He studied first the one in the bush jacket whom he had shot himself. He stripped the body, searching the clothes swiftly but thoroughly with all the skill of a man trained and experienced in locating hidden objects. He turned to the naked body itself and finally extracted a slender steel needle from under the skin over the dead man's shoulder blade. He slipped the needle into a hidden slot in his ragged sandals, then turned to the beaten and tortured man executed with the single shot to his head.

Even his cool eyes seemed to wince as he saw the extent of the dead civilian's injuries. But they were the eyes of a man who had seen much of what man can inflict on his fellowman, and he went back to his work of searching this body. He came up with a thin wallet and took a card from the wallet. He stared at the blood-smeared card for some time. Then his quick eyes looked past the card and the dead man to the ground under the corpse's right hand. There in the hard dust and dirt, the executed man had traced a single word in his own blood:

MAMBA

TWO

Across the vast, dusty African plain, hazy purple mountains towering barren in the distance, the stream of refugees stumbled toward the sprawling relief camps. Here there was at least the hope of food, and if they died, it would be among people, not alone in the brush of some empty canyon like an animal.

His "blind" eyes rolled up to the pitiless sun, the tattered peasant who had stalked the patrol and killed the civilian in the clearing limped into the camp with the other eager refugees. Once inside among the prefabricated buildings and tents that stretched as far as the eye could see, he staggered away to wander alone through the buildings until he reached the main camp administration building. He seemed to stumble aimlessly up the steps into the unpainted prefab.

Inside the office, a large, red-faced man with stunned eyes sat at a desk behind a nameplate that read James Donovan, U.S. Aid Service. He, Donovan, looked up wearily as the apparition in its ragged clothes and dirty turban staggered in.

"I'm sorry," he said in careful English, "but you can't come in here unless you have business."

The peasant grinned through the dust and dirt caked into his black face, and began to unwind his filthy turban.

"What are you doing!" Donovan cried. "I told you, you can't come in here!"

The peasant had his turban off now, and held the dirty cloth around a pair of high-powered binoculars.

"Dammit, I don't speak Amharic! Why didn't they send someone here who spoke Amharic! Listen, you can't—"

Donovan stopped. He stared at the tattered "native" whose thick dark hair was cut short in Western fashion. Still grinning, the "refugee" began to use the turban cloth to wipe his face. Sunburned Caucasian skin emerged from beneath the black. A pair of cold, amused eyes watched Donovan's astonishment.

"I'll take the rest off later when I get a shower," the "peasant" said. "Now I need some assistance. You are Donovan, right? I'll need identification from you to—"

"Identification? Assistance?" Donovan sputtered, blinking. "Who the hell are you? What are you doing here? I'll have to report—"

"No report," the cold-eyed stranger said. He reached under his ragged white clothes and held out a card. "CRA-5. Is that enough? And don't tell me you're not at least a CIA field contact."

Donovan looked at the card. He didn't take it. He stood up and walked into a back room. The disguised man followed him into the room where there were two desks and two telephones. Donovan sat on the edge of one of the desks.

"Okay, you're Nigel Connors, CIA. I'm to give you all the assistance I can. I don't like it, Connors. I'm here to help starving people, not spy on their government or their rebellion. But I work for my country, and if the

Company needs me, I'm supposed to help. So go ahead, what do you want?''

"Later, first, a shower and some clothes. Right now, a tight lip and to be left alone in here.''

"My pleasure,'' Donovan said, and he left the room, closing the door loudly behind him. Not everyone in the government liked playing the spy for the CIA.

The "refugee'' stood for a time, motionless and listening. Donovan had not stopped outside the door, and no one else was around the rickety prefab. Satisfied, he sat down at one of the desks, picked up the telephone receiver, and dialed a series of numbers. There was a long pause, then many clicks and squawks on the phone. Then a soft, sultry voice answered.

"N3, Killmaster, Nick Carter. What is your pleasure, N3?''

The damned computer. Nick Carter grinned in the empty room. Hawk's little joke, that voice.

"Code-X, sweetheart,'' Carter said. "David Hawk, *muy pronto, por favor*.''

"Code-X computing,'' the voice purred. "And interface in English, N3; you are coded Emergency Only for Spanish.''

Carter grinned as he waited, calculating the time in Washington, D.C. The distant city seemed light-years away, but it was only eight hours by the clock. It was 4:00 A.M. where Hawk would be awakened by the insistent ringing beside his bed and pick up the receiver and bark angrily.

"It's about time, N3! But it could have waited until six o'clock when you're three days overdue!''

"And a good morning to you, sir,'' Carter said cheerfully, wiping more of the black pigment from his tanned face along with the sweat in the stifling Eritrean midafternoon heat.

"Well? Yes or no?"

"Yes," Carter said. "Would I call if it were no?"

"You've been known to."

"Not on this kind of sale."

"Dead? No question?"

"Took his pulse myself."

"The documents?"

"In a needle under his skin. Safe and sound."

"Who was he selling to this time?"

"The Ethiopians. Or rather, the Ethiopian general Meni Haile Tenamu, in case he's working for himself— which is pretty damned possible. And, of course, the Ethiopians could be transmitting the stuff on to almost anyone, but probably Moscow."

"Of course it's going on to Moscow," Hawk growled in his dark bedroom. "So he was in his Soviet phase. All right, well done, N3. I hate all triple agents. You can't depend on them."

"Not like a good, solid double agent."

"Exactly. Now, can I get some sleep?"

"I'm not sure," Carter said.

In the sweltering room he mopped his face, wiped off streaks of the black makeup, and waited. One ear was alert to any sounds around the building that could signal danger or eavesdropping; the other waited for Hawk to digest the fact that Carter had something more to talk about. He heard the click of his boss's butane lighter in the far-off Alexandria, Virginia, bedroom. He could almost smell the stink of the cheap cigar that was Hawk's only vice and one of his few pleasures.

"What have you got, Nick?"

Carter told him what had happened in the remote clearing in the Eritrean mountains. "He had a secret CIA identity card. A CIA man in medium cover, I had no alert he was working in the same area. I don't know what he was doing in Eritrea or how he got into General Tenamu's hands. All I know is that Tenamu wanted something from him he didn't get, and so he killed him.''

There was a long pause, and the sound of smoke being blown in the faraway dark room.

"I had no alert CIA was in there either, N3. Give me the ID number."

Carter gave it to him. "Sir? He didn't die instantly. He hung on just long enough to write a word in his own blood in the dirt."

"What word?"

" 'Mamba.' "

"That's all? 'Mamba'?"

"That's it."

Carter could almost smell the cloud of smoke around Hawk's head and see him scowling in the darkness.

"All right, I'll pass it on to the CIA. It's not our problem, but as a matter of courtesy . . ."

"Honor among thieves?" Carter laughed.

"Something like that. Take a day off, Nick. Have a good vacation, then be in Cairo tomorrow for reassignment."

"I might even take two days," Carter said, and hung up.

He sat in that hot back room of the prefabricated temporary building for a long time. He imagined Hawk swearing as the line went dead. It was a game they played, he and Hawk, but there was more than a game behind it. Hawk wanted the discipline of the engineer, the control of a computer over his organization. Carter wanted the freedom of the artist, the unpredictableness that made him the top agent in the supersecret AXE unit, the freedom to, from time to time, follow a whim.

Carter let out a deep, slow sigh, and decided that right now his whim was for a shower—long and hot and soapy. Endless soap and hot water. A kind of lethargy hung over him as it always did at the end of an assignment, a killing or any other. With an effort of will, he roused himself and stood up.

He walked out of the steambath of the back room, the dust that blew in through all the cracks of the prefab gritty under his bare feet. The American camp administrator, Donovan, was still at his desk. He looked curiously at Carter now.

"Get done what you wanted?"

"Thanks," Carter said. "Now all I need is a hot shower and some clothes."

"Don't I wish," Donovan said. "That's going to be harder than calling Washington, or whatever you did in there. All we have here is hard work and sweat and vodka. A lot more vodka than water, believe me. Clothes I can get you, but a vodka rubdown's the best I can do for a bath. Try it—you might get to like it."

"No, thanks—the vodka comes later. Where *do* I find a shower?"

"Well, you could try for Asmara, but I wouldn't advise it. A plane leaves for Addis Ababa almost every two hours. That's your best bet."

"Where do I get this plane?"

"Other end of camp, the flats. Anyone in a jeep'll take you there. I'd do it myself, but I've got a delegation of hungry elders to soothe in ten minutes. It's not even a bad walk, but you'd better borrow a hat or put that turban back on."

"How are you going to soothe hungry elders?"

"Food would be best. But since about half the

shipments never seem to show up from Addis or anywhere else, I'll see what some judicious lying, deceit and chicanery can do.''

"Good luck," Carter said.

Donovan only shrugged, and Carter wrapped his turban around his head again and stepped out into the murderous sun. His face was streaked black and white where he had rubbed off the dark makeup, but he didn't worry about it; the refugees were too hungry to notice, the camp personnel too busy.

He threaded his way through the starving Eritreans. They sat on the parched ground with their emaciated arms, skeletal ribs and shoulders, and bloated bellies. The young and the old, large-eyed, gentle as dying cattle. Some were so weak they only stared ahead from fixed, blind eyes, even hope gone. Some huddled in the shade of the tents, out of the merciless sun. A few, stronger and angrier, milled about in gesticulating groups, their emaciated black arms waving like the struggling feet of some enormous black-and-white beetle helpless on its back.

The two men appeared from out of a larger group gathered near a gate to listen to an unseen high-voiced speaker exhorting them to some action that probably would not be favorable to the camp authorities: two thick-armed, well-fed, compact men in gray uniforms without insignia carrying assault rifles—AK-47 Kalishnikovs. Bush slouch hats, paratrooper boots, sidearms, canteens, ammunition belts. The works.

And it was not the natives they had come for.

Carter plunged into the nearest tent.

The first fusillade tore rents in the tent, spewed the blood and bone of two old men who had been sitting on cots out of the sun over the other screaming refugees in the tent, shattered the center pole, and collapsed the tent on the dead and the screaming and the terrified hidden under cots.

Through the canvas and rope, through the shouting and milling mob of the starving, the two well-fed men in gray clubbed and cursed their way. The dying natives were frantic not to die, not at that moment. Hopeless, they were not going to be killed ahead of time. They scattered, panicked, blocking each other and the two attackers.

From the collapsed tent, Carter snaked through the blindly surging mob. The administration building was a hundred yards ahead. He reached the shelter of a row of storage huts and the camp's single infirmary where a line of women and children waited, and jumped up to run for the administration building.

The single shots came from two directions at once: one from behind one of the tents on the left, the other from near a storehouse building on the right. Or near those places. Carter, running crouched and weaving, had seen no one and nothing. Not even movement.

Just two quick shots from the high-powered rifles.

The first burned through the fleshy part of his left bicep. A near miss. It saved his life. The second bullet, a split second later, grazed his ear as he spun left from the impact of the first.

Blood pulsed slowly out of his arm down his ragged white robes.

From the spin to the left he twisted into a backward lunge against his momentum, hitting the ground hard on his right shoulder as two more shots tore the empty air where he would have been if he had completed the spin.

Whoever they were, they had shot at people before.

He rolled left over his bleeding arm.

The shots hit behind him.

Although trained, they were not too experienced, both shooting at the same place. If they had each taken one side to shoot at, Carter would be dead.

A somersault backward gave him the cover of a corrugated metal storage building.

Two bullets hit, one on each side of where he had been.

They were learning.

Crouching next to the corrugated Quonset hut, Carter quickly assembled his sniper rifle. He threw away the telescopic sight and fixed a short, thin bayonet to the muzzle, all the time watching with one eye the open space in front and on both sides. One eye surveyed the half circle while he assembled and loaded the rifle. Only a half circle: there had not been time for them to be behind him. Not yet.

Unless there were more than the two of them.

You have to take some risks. Do the possible and a little more and forget the rest. If there were more and they were behind him, he'd trust to luck. For the two in front, he'd have to rely on more than luck.

Carter watched the space between the corrugated Quonset and the tents on the right, the building on the left. Alone in the whole camp. No one in sight. The refugees might be starving to death, but they weren't fools. They knew about guns. They somehow found the strength to get away, hide, go to cover.

The rifle ready, open space empty, enemy unlocated, Carter checked his ordnance: Hugo securely up the voluminous sleeve of his white rags; Pierre tight to his upper thigh under the torn, baggy native trousers; Wilhelmina neatly secured to the small of his back; rifle in hand. Ammo? Ammo low, but possibly sufficient. One bandolier of clips for the sniper rifle. An extra half-dozen 9mm clips for Wilhelmina in various parts of the rags and his anatomy. Hugo sharp and Pierre fully gassed.

A movement on the left.

Small, no more than a flicker at the corner of a tent limp under the airless scorching sun.

He steadied the sights of his rifle on the open space between the point of the movement and the next tent, on where, if he guessed right, the man would be next as he tried to circle and get behind Carter.

The man ran into view, frozen momentarily in Carter's line of sight.

Then he was gone with the echo of Carter's shot and a spot of red widening on his gray shoulder. Only the empty space remained—and a patch of moist red far-off on the dirt between the two tents. Bulls-eye.

The movement on the right was slower, behind a wheeled metal wagon used to collect trash and bodies in the camp. There was no clear shot; it was time to retreat.

Only there was nowhere to retreat.

There was nothing behind him but the edge of the camp, the fence, and the vast open plain baking in heat and dust.

Carter heard the helicopter.

A small, single-rotor chopper was coming in low from the east and the mountains. Carter heard the helicopter and another sound: the clank and grind of tracked vehicles. Gun-carriers or personnel carriers. Soldiers. Probably whistled up by Donovan.

The chopper was closer. It came in very low across the edge of the camp, banked, circled back, and dropped down into the dust. The two gunmen in gray dashed from their cover and climbed aboard.

The helicopter began to rise, carrying the gunmen to their escape.

THREE

The helicopter struggled ten feet off the ground. One skid had hooked a long tent rope. The pilot shouted above the roar of the rotor at the two gunmen, pointing down to the rope. The chopper swung back and forth, pulling again and again. It collapsed the tent and dragged it as the two gunmen tried to lean down and free the rope.

The sound of the approaching tracked vehicles on the far side of the camp came closer. There was no way the gunmen were going to be able to reach the rope and free it, and the wild swerves of the helicopter refused to shake it loose.

Carter saw the long rope at the other side of the tent. A jeep was parked next to the collapsed tent. Quickly he looped the rope around the jeep's bumper, secured it with a half hitch, and jumped into the jeep just as the helicopter pilot waved the gunman back inside the helicopter and gave it full throttle.

The chopper lifted the tent clear, headed west toward the mountains, and shuddered and swooped violently as the weight of the jeep hit it through the taut ropes and dangling tent. The pilot fought the controls and shouted at the gunmen again. They looked back, seeing the jeep and Carter. Their rifles appeared.

Carter looked for the keys. They weren't there. He dropped behind the dashboard as the gunmen opened fire and shattered the windshield. Wilhelmina in hand, Carter leaned out and fired back. The gunmen ducked out of sight inside the chopper. The pilot cast one furious glance back at Carter and the jeep, and then, low to the ground, surged to full power. The helicopter didn't have the muscle to lift the jeep, but it had enough to drag the rope, the collapsed tent, the jeep and Carter out through the fence and away across the dusty plain toward the nearest foothills to the east.

The jeep careened wildly as the helicopter pulled it first right then left in an attempt to shake the rope or the jeep or both, then roared straight ahead, bouncing the jeep off rocks and gullies, thorn bushes, and low hillocks. Carter leaned out with Wilhelmina and tried to get a shot at the chopper's engine.

The gunmen's heads appeared, and their Kalishnikovs. They fired back at the jeep.

Neither side could get a clear shot.

Carter had to pull his head in whenever the gunmen fired from the helicopter. With one hand hanging onto the jeep, he could only fire with his Luger.

The gunmen in the chopper had to try to balance the weaving of the chopper with the careening of the jeep and duck Carter's fire at the same time.

The standoff went on as the helicopter dragged the jeep and Carter across the hard, dry, dusty land closer and closer to the foothills.

Then Carter saw it ahead.

A giant Soviet earth-moving machine. Part of the USSR's aid to the Provisional Military Administrative Council of Ethiopia. What it was there to build Carter didn't know and the helicopter pilot didn't care. The chopper swerved left and straight toward the giant earth-mover with its gray painted body and gigantic wheels. Red stars and steel arms. Lifts and back-hoes and scoops.

The pilot would use the gigantic piece of equipment to knock the jeep, or Carter, loose from the helicopter. Or threaten to do that. There was no way the jeep could hit the earth-mover without the risk of catching and pulling the helicopter down. The pilot had to get close enough to make Carter jump out of the jeep to avoid being smashed into the giant machine, but not so close that the jeep would hook to the earth-mover and drag the helicopter down.

It was a nice calculation—close enough to force Carter to jump, but not so close that the jeep would actually hit the earth-mover.

Carter held to the jeep, calculating the distance that closed rapidly as the helicopter flew closer and closer to the giant piece of equipment that loomed like a cliff almost higher than the altitude of the helicopter itself.

He waited.

The helicopter flew closer.

The giant gray and red earth-mover filled the whole sky.

Carter waited.

The white face of the pilot looked back.

Carter waited.

The pilot flew straight on, staring back at Carter second to second.

The pilot had to turn.

Carter waited, then jumped.

He tumbled from the moving jeep, hit hard on his shoulder, and felt the searing pain in his wounded arm. He rolled and came up on his feet, then tucked his head down and rolled again on the wounded arm, feeling the blood spurt from the bullet hole. Then he got to his feet and sprawled into a thorn bush that ripped like fire.

He sprawled and heard the thunderous crash of metal against metal.

Carter smiled before he passed out.

The voices were inside his head. Gibberish. "The Murders in the Rue Morgue." Ape voices. Jabbering . . . jabbering. . . .

Carter opened his eyes.

He didn't move. He lay utterly motionless. The voices were almost on top of him. And the gibberish of his dream was Amharic. Four voices. Or five. Laughing.

Without moving anything but his eyes, Carter studied where he was. Thick branches and leathery leaves were above and all around him. A large rock rested against his head like a pillow. The shadow of a dirt wall cut off sun and light to his left. A riverbank! A stream. He was in thick bushes at the bottom of some kind of dry watercourse. He was totally hidden under a thick thorn bush at the bottom of a rocky stream bed.

The voices were to his left, up above the bank. There were at least five, possibly more.

Very slowly, Carter moved his head to the right, then to the left. It was a narrow dry watercourse, open to the right but shadowed under the undercut bank to his left.

He listened.

The voices were close but at least ten yards away up on the plain itself. Talking and laughing. As if on a break, a rest stop. He pictured them in his mind, seated and lying on the hard dirt, lounging, not alert.

Carefully he rolled his whole body to his left, making no sound, his eye on the lip of the watercourse bank, his right hand on Wilhelmina. His left arm had stopped bleeding; his left shoulder throbbed but wasn't broken. Doubling up almost into a ball, then opening himself up, he inched out from under the thorny brush and moved closer to the riverbank shadow in a series of opening and closing motions like an inchworm on its side.

Once under the bank he rocked himself up to a kneeling position. He was extremely cautious, moving nothing in the shallow stream bed, not even a pebble. He found the thickness of a dusty bush, turned his head sideways, and slowly raised himself until one eye could peer through the base of the brush.

There were five Ethiopian soldiers lounging on the hard dirt and waiting. Waiting like any soldiers in any army anywhere. Waiting, doing nothing they didn't have to, talking of furloughs and nights on the town. In English, Swahili or their Amharic.

"You had better forget that lady, Mushara. With our general on the ass of our lieutenant, we're going nowhere."

"But I must have a night! She was magnificent."

Another laughed. "To Mushi they are all magnificent. I remember the time there was this toothless whore in Harar, and Mushara brought her incense, took her to a restaurant!"

They all had a good laugh on Mushara. But it didn't last long as the first speaker's prophecy about their immediate future depressed them.

"What does the general think, that these in the

helicopter are those who shot the Russian this morning?''

"Them or the one they pursue."

"The general is afraid of his shadow."

"He should be, the stealing he does."

"Bah! Who does not steal in the high command?"

"But this general steals more than most."

"And sends it away to buy friends, eh, Mushara?"

"Shhh! The lieutenant."

With another soldier, the officer Carter had seen leading the patrol that morning came trotting through the brush. He motioned abruptly, and the five resting soldiers gathered to squat around him like tribesmen with their spears. You can put anyone into a uniform, but it isn't always easy to make him into a soldier.

"The helicopter has crashed ahead beyond the Russian machine, but we have seen no bodies. There is also no body near the shattered jeep. And there is no one alive either. But there are construction buildings ahead where we are building an airfield. Therefore, I am certain the three in the helicopter have captured the one in the jeep and are hiding in those buildings. The general wishes us to capture at least one of these people. We—"

The barrage of deadly automatic fire came from three sides, a semicircle of attack in the brush with the seven soldiers caught against the flat line of the dry watercourse where Carter crouched.

FOUR

It lasted no more than a minute.

The blood of all seven drenched the brush along the watercourse. Blood and flesh spattered across the hard dirt, the bushes, and Carter himself hidden down below the bank of the dry stream. Their screams and cries of agony and dying moans echoed across the soundless plain where there was no one to hear.

No one except the three killers in gray uniforms who came walking slowly, warily out of the brush to look down at the seven dead bodies. One was still crawling. The shorter of the three attackers shot him in the head, then went on to the next. The helicopter pilot looked at his watch.

"They're plenty dead. Let's go," he said.

"I like to make sure," the shorter gunman replied. He had a bandaged shoulder where Carter had winged him as he'd dashed between buildings earlier in the camp.

They were speaking English!

"If we have to walk, it could take us hours. And it

gets hot out here," the pilot said.

"Enough, Emil," the taller one said. "There are buildings ahead. Perhaps we can find something there."

Obviously the leader, the taller one turned and started off across the broiling dusty plain. All three wore caps now, with long sun visors and neck coverings. They were prepared for marching under the African sun.

In the watercourse Carter struggled to his feet. He had lost his sniper rifle when he jumped from the jeep, and now had only Wilhelmina.

He moved through the dry brush of the narrow watercourse that cut across the plain past the gray Soviet earth-mover.

He saw the helicopter, down and battered, but it had not crashed hard or burned. The pilot knew his work, just as the two ambushers did. They were trained men, maybe not overly imaginative or original, but with enough training to learn fast in action. The pilot had made one mistake and hit the giant earth-mover, but he had not made another in attempting to pull the jeep free. He had eased back in time, stalled, and dropped onto the chopper's skids. It wouldn't fly again for a while, but the three men had walked away and ambushed the Ethiopian patrol. Now they had gone off across the dusty plain, finished with Carter.

But Carter wasn't finished with them.

He saw them now in the distance nearing a row of temporary buildings. There were other earth-movers, and graders, and trucks. Someone was building an airstrip. There were four low prefabs. Carter heard the shots. Four shots, and all from the direction of the buildings.

He got up and broke into a ground-covering trot along the narrow watercourse. As he neared the row of silent buildings he heard a motor start. A truck motor from the sound of it. He peered over the edge of the watercourse but saw nothing. The sound was coming from behind the row of buildings. Carter ducked down and circled the buildings until he was in the rear.

Over the rim of the gully he saw the three. They stood between a covered Soviet truck and the wall of the last building. Four men faced them, their hands in the air. Across the distance Carter could see other men sprawled on the ground. The bodies and the four with their hands up wore Ethiopian army uniforms.

The shots broke the vast stillness of the plain, echoing off the nearby foothills. In the distance the four men with their hands up fell sprawling backward, shot in cold blood where they stood with their hands up. As Carter watched, the two gunmen walked from one to the other of the fallen men and carefully shot each one in the head. The bodies jerked spasmodically and lay still. The two gunmen in gray didn't take chances on survivors.

Carter slipped up over the edge of the watercourse and began to crawl closer. It was slow and hot under the scorching African sun, and he hadn't reached the first buildings when he heard the truck engine start again and saw the three killers jump into the cab and drive off across the dusty plain toward the nearest line of hills.

Eleven bloody bodies lay sprawled in the dust all around the silent row of construction buildings, their empty eyes staring up at the blazing sky. Carter bent down to each one to see if there was anything he could do, but they were all dead. Five were Ethiopian soldiers, four looked as if they had been Ethiopian civilians, and two were Caucasians with pronounced Slavic features.

He searched the two Caucasians and came out with

fat wallets. Both were Russian civil engineers. Road builders. Road builders and soldiers, a major and a captain. Both had probably breathed a sigh of relief when they got sent to Ethiopia and not Afghanistan.

He found what he wanted at the far end of the last building. The motor pool. There were three Soviet trucks and two American jeeps. The escaping attackers had not bothered to sabotage them. After slaughtering everyone they had found, they had not expected any close pursuit.

Carter found a rack of rifles and some ammunition in the motor pool office. He used his ignition tool to start a jeep and went after the attackers who had now become his quarry. He would have the element of surprise and one other advantage: both vehicles would move ahead of their clouds of dust. He would be hidden from them by their own dust cloud, as thick behind them as any smoke screen.

He picked up the dust cloud some five miles after leaving the buildings. They moved steadily toward the foothills. He drove as fast as possible over the rough terrain, and closed the gap between them. He wanted to reach them before they could get lost in the mountains. They were still some miles from the first slopes of tree-shadowed hills when he saw that he wouldn't. The cloud of dust ahead began to move a lot faster. They had spotted him at last.

Carter pushed the accelerator to the floor, and the jeep slewed and bounced off the mounds and ridges of the rugged plain. Ahead the fleeing truck suddenly appeared as it reached the foothills and the cloud of dust dissipated.

Then Carter was in the foothills, winding up a broad canyon between tree-lined slopes. The truck, heavier and wider, was forced to slow as the canyon narrowed between great boulders and the hard dirt track wound like a corkscrew. Carter rapidly closed the gap. Steering with his knees, he aimed the rifle and shot out the rear tires of the careening truck.

With a wild ripping of metal, the truck hurled off the road and crashed through the trees, shearing off whole trunks until it shuddered to a stop against a tree too thick to break. Carter skidded the jeep ten yards behind the crashed truck. The two gunmen in gray uniforms jumped out. Carter shot one of them in the leg, sending him spinning into the brush. The second fired back. Carter ducked behind a boulder. He heard the gunmen crashing away up the narrow dirt track, going deeper into the hills.

Carter slipped out from behind the rock and ran soundlessly past the truck. The helicopter pilot lay crushed behind the wheel, the steering post protruding in dark blood and broken ribs from his back.

A trail of blood led up along the path. His trained eyes knew from the blood that the gunmen wouldn't get far unless the wounded one was abandoned by his partner.

He ran on. He wanted them alive. At least one of them.

Two shots showered leaves down over him.

Prone, he returned the fire high, and watched.

Two more shots exploded from ahead, one fifty yards up behind two boulders to the left of the dirt track, and the other another ten yards farther along behind a thick tree to the right of the track. He steadied his rifle on the nearer enemy, held it with one hand, and fired Wilhelmina with the other hand.

Another two shots cracked from up ahead. Carter

fired the rifle with one hand. The man, caught for an instant raised-up and firing, screamed and fell kicking and flopping out onto the dirt road. A red stain appeared in the center of his forehead. His kicking and thrashing slowly stopped like a fish out of water dying in gasps for breath that would never come.

The second gunman abandoned his cover and ran on up the road. Carter pursued him, noting the bloody shoulder and leg wounds on his recent victim. The escaping attacker was the unwounded one. Carter saw him running wildly up the road, all cover abandoned. Carter smiled coldly; everyone had his panic level. He aimed carefully for the fleeing man's legs—and the whole hillside ahead erupted into a volley of gunfire.

Carter dived for cover.

Bullets whined and ripped through the trees and off the rocks, shattering the sky and echoing through the entire canyon. Carter huddled behind a rock, his face pressed to the dirt. He counted, estimating there were at least twenty-five guns, AK-47s from the sound, but mixed with M-16s and even some Sten and Uzi guns.

Then it stopped.

The silence was almost touchable, a physical shape filling the narrow canyon still echoing to the dying sounds of the fusillade.

Carter raised himself up.

He saw them far off, all in gray uniforms, the one fleeing attacker now among them, pointing back. He heard the helicopters. Six of them, large choppers. Mixed Soviet and American. Troop carriers. Gunships. The gray-uniformed soldiers clambered aboard, and they lifted off one by one until only one chopper was left. One lone man stood on a high rock looking down toward where Carter lay hidden.

He stood imperious, without fear. Across the distance Carter could just make out his face: a cold, hard face, like some mountain eagle. Slim and narrow, lined and craggy, white hair under his blue beret, a thick gray mustache. A gaunt face, commanding.

Then he climbed into the last helicopter and was gone.

Alone in the silent canyon among the dry Ethiopian mountains, Carter slowly stood up, held his shoulder where the bleeding had stopped, and looked toward where the helicopters had disappeared. He stood staring long after their motors had died away.

FIVE

Dawn comes painfully over the human mass that is Cairo.

Nick Carter stood on the high balcony and felt the awakening of the city like the slow, ponderous stirrings of some giant, bloated slug squeezed in its narrow valley between the desert and the Nile.

Alone on the balcony of the luxury hotel, he felt the hot morning sweat on his bare chest and his bandaged shoulder, and lit a cigarette and watched the sky turn pink across the City of the Dead. A hundred thousand people lived in the medieval tombs, raising families beside the graves of Mameluke rulers. Minarets and domes thrust up behind the ancient mausoleums, with modern high-rises beyond, and in the far distance were the baked stone hills of the desert that surrounded the city.

"Nikita?"

The hot whisper was in his ear. A low, soft, throaty whisper like the purr of a thick-furred cat in heat. Her graceful arms were around his neck, her heavy, swaying breasts pressed against his naked back, her belly hard and tight to his buttocks.

"You will catch cold, Niki."

Her mouth on his neck kissed softly, licking and biting. Laughing. He picked her up and carried her back into the room. She buried her face in his neck, nibbling on his skin with sharp teeth like a hungry vampire, squirming in his arms. His wound ached, but not too much.

"You don't love me, Nikita," she teased. "You leave me alone in the bed."

"I must have been crazy," Carter said.

He placed her on the bed. A long, lean woman with the pale snow skin of northern forests. Lean and long, but with the full wide hips of a woman, the heavy breasts thick and soft as she lay looking up at him with pale blue eyes in the dim light of the dawn bedroom high above the city. Breasts that lay soft and massive and yet somehow thrust taut, the pink nipples hard and excited.

"A fool," she whispered on the bed below him. A king-size bed torn apart and ravaged, its sheets flung into twisted piles through the two nights they had been there.

"Insane," he said as he kneeled in the morning light and buried his face in her breasts, buried his face down into the wedge of pale blond hair.

"Life is so brief." She twisted around him, kissing the hard body that throbbed under her lips.

"So little time." He spread her legs wide, kneeled, and looked at her.

"You are waiting perhaps for the permission of the Politburo?"

She lay back, spreading her legs even wider, raising them toward the ceiling, then back over his shoulders, and he went down to her, into her, as she locked her arms behind him and gasped for breath beneath his chest as he thrust and thrust and thrust . . . .

The sun was hazy beyond the gauzy curtains across the balcony door when Carter finally smiled down into her aquamarine eyes. She looked up at him, tracing a finger over his chest, watching him, playing with his body lightly, slowly.

"I have to go," she said.

"So soon?"

She kissed him. "I know. Only two days. What can I say? The Kremlin is a hard taskmaster, Nikita. Not soft and luxurious like the U.N. We must work! Strive! Sweat!"

He rolled her over and pressed his hands slowly down her spine. "But we've got a lot still to do here, Anna Ivanovna . . ."

She moaned into the pillow. "With you there is always a lot still to do. Oh . . . Nikita!" His hands came around her hips to rest between her thighs, but his fingers did not remain still for long. "You can't work at the U.N. You're not human. A satyr . . . a . . . Oh . . . Oh . . ."

An hour later she opened her eyes, sighed slowly, and sat up. He lay on his back in the silent bedroom of her apartment in the luxury hotel, watching her. She smiled at him, then kissed him lightly.

"Niki, I really must go now. I am sorry. The boss must not be more late than her subordinates."

"I'll miss you."

"No, but you are sweet to say it." She traced a pattern on his belly. "You are a nice man—for an American and a U.N. robot."

"And you are a wonderful woman for the Chief of Transport for USSR Aid to the Government of Ethiopia."

"A very long title and not even a KGB agent." She hit his leg playfully. "You had me checked out."

"True, I admit it. The only Russian foreign executive I ever met who wasn't KGB."

"True, I admit it."

They both laughed and kissed, and then Anna Ivanovna Strelskov got up and went into the bathroom to shower. Carter lay in bed and closed his eyes, listening to the sounds rising from the teeming city far below. The voices of twelve million human beings screaming for a share of life. For the smallest share of what he and Anna Ivanovna had in this quiet, clean, secure room.

He listened to her singing in the shower. Two days away from it all. Away from the needs and demands of those teeming millions and their rulers. Isolated in this room, safe because he had checked her out and she had checked him out. She was not a KGB agent, and he knew he had checked clean as Nicholas Meyer, U.N. employee. He always did; AXE made sure of that.

Two days, but now she had her work and he had his. He grinned in the big, silent bedroom as he thought of David Hawk. The irascible head of AXE would be chewing his foul cigars in fury by now. When Hawk said take a day off he did not mean two days.

"You are thinking," she said. She stood in the bathroom door, damp and naked, a towel wrapped turban-fashion around her hair. "Since when does a U.N. employee think?"

"Ever since they started making us work with Soviet executives," Carter said with a grin. "Finished?"

She sighed, then came over and kissed his belly. "No, but I must deny myself. Tonight?"

"Maybe."

"Ah?" She smiled. "No strings, *da*? The shower, at least, is now yours."

He took his shower. Hot and scalding, then ice cold. Two days in bed with Anna Ivanovna had built a strange, distant haze in his mind, and he needed a clear head to talk to Hawk. Drying, he came out and watched her putting a final hairpin into the gleaming blond chignon at the base of her neck as she checked herself in the long mirror. A severe linen business suit, the Soviet arbiters and rulers as conservative as ever.

"Only maybe?" Anna Ivanovna asked, turning with that brisk movement that precedes the opening of a door to leave. "Tonight?"

"Definitely," Carter said. Let Hawk wait another day.

She smiled, blew him a kiss, and left the suite.

The shots exploded. The room shook. The bullets tore through the closed door.

Wilhelmina was in his hand from the hidden compartment in his overnight bag.

He flung open the door, flattening himself to the wall.

Frightened voices. Hysteria somewhere. No doors opened along the corridor. This was Cairo.

A long, empty corridor. Except for Anna Ivanovna.

She lay sprawled on her back on the thick carpeting, blood oozing from her elegant body, her suit darkening with the blood that soaked into it.

At the far end of the corridor the fire door was still ajar. Carter fired four shots through the door—middle and low. Nothing happened. The assassin was gone. He bent over Anna Ivanovna. Her blue eyes looked up at him, already going empty. Pain in the eyes, and fear, and a kind of reproach. She saw the Luger in his hand.

"You . . . lied . . . to me . . . Nikita."

"I'm sorry," Carter said.

"I did not lie, but you lied. It was you they wanted dead, not me. Now I'm dead. Tonight . . . will . . . have to . . . wait . . ."

"Anna . . ."

She reached slowly and touched his muscled naked body as he knelt in the corridor.

"So . . . beautiful . . ."

And she was dead.

Carter remained crouched there for a moment. Then he stood and strode to the fire door. Spent shells littered the floor: AK-47 shells. From the look of it, one man had fired at the person who came out of the suite door. Anna was not KGB, so it was not meant for her. Someone was out to kill him. But Anna Ivanovna was dead.

Doors were open a crack now. Fearful eyes stared out. Far below there were sirens. Naked, Carter hurried back to her room, dressed quickly, zipped up his overnight bag, and took the AXE-designed escape device from the heel of a shoe.

On the balcony he attached the thin wire, lowered himself over the edge, and dropped two balconies down to an empty one. He retrieved the unit, repacked it, and walked through the empty suite and out to the elevator. He rode down to the lobby, walked back to the linen supply room, picked the lock on the side door into the service alley, and walked out to the street to blend with the hordes of pedestrians who fought the bumper-to-bumper traffic for the right of way.

One of the last of the once-famous sidewalk cafés was across the teeming street from the hotel. Carter took a table, ordered coffee, and asked for a telephone. Through the passing mass of people in Western clothes, in the long robes and headdresses of the villages, in every possible dress, he watched the door of the hotel where the police were checking everyone who came out.

His coffee and telephone came. He sipped the thick

Turkish brew and dialed the secret code that would connect him to the AXE computer.

"Good morning, N3," the soft, caressing voice Hawk had given the computer said. "Mr. Hawk has been expecting you."

"I'll bet he has, honey," Carter said, but his heart wasn't in to joking with the disembodied voice. "Put me through."

Clicks, pauses, pings, beeps, and silence.

"You'd better be calling from prison, a hospital, or the morgue," Hawk growled. "When I say a day I mean a day, N3. Even for you."

Carter watched the police at the door of the hotel through the bedlam, watched the covered stretcher with its body bag come out.

"The lady I spent the last two days with has just been murdered by someone who wanted to kill me. She was a very nice lady. Russian. Intelligent. Beautiful. Nonpolitical. She's dead not because of what she did but because of what I do. I left her lying in her own blood on the floor of a hotel corridor so I could remain unknown, so I could call you. She deserved better."

There was a long silence at the far end of the line, finally broken by the sound of a butane lighter.

"All right, Nick. Any ideas who?"

"No, but it was the second try in three days." Carter told his boss about the attack at the Ethiopian relief camp and his escape. "No ID, but I know they weren't Ethiopian government soldiers or rebels. They're trained and experienced, but not real veterans. Well equipped, plenty of helicopters. They didn't want witnesses. They were after me and no one else."

"They knew you were in the camp," Hawk decided. "They penetrated the disguise."

"Not necessarily. No one except you knew I was in

that camp, and even you didn't know for sure I'd be there until I called in."

"You're saying that no one there knew who you were in time to have called them up."

"That's how I read the signs," Carter agreed, "and that means I had to have been tailed or identified by someone that day, locally."

"And that means the attacks have to be connected to the agent you eliminated, the Ethiopian general, or the dead CIA man."

"I don't see any other answer."

There was silence on the line. Carter watched the ambulance take away Anna Ivanovna. The police huddled in front of the hotel doors, obviously not happy. He had been sure no one had seen him enter the hotel with Anna Ivanovna, but someone must have. If the attacker had found him, sooner or later the police would. Most probably later, knowing the Egyptian police. Probably a lot later if the attacker had silenced his informant, which he almost certainly had.

"That murdered CIA operative was top secret, hush-hush," Hawk's distant voice said slowly. "He was working on a major bind for the U.S. You're aware of the size and diversity of our international aid programs? Both funds and food?"

"Give or take a few billion."

"Well, a great deal of what's going to Africa—perhaps most of it—isn't reaching its destinations. That's being kept under wraps, but everyone in Africa knows about it, and our image and interest is being badly damaged. There are rumors it's all a U.S. scam —that the food and cash are never sent at all. It's a big scheme to weaken black Africa in favor of our buddy South Africa. Follow me?"

"Cute," Carter said. "The man they killed was working on it?"

"Under cover."

"So our Ethiopian general must be involved, and that's why they killed the CIA man."

"One possibility."

"What's another?"

There was a long pause at the far end of the line in predawn Virginia. "For a number of years, N3, we have had very deep cover reports of an elite mercenary force based somewhere in Africa who works for anyone who pays high enough. The code word talked about is 'Mamba.' Elite jobs, hard hits, in and out where no one else goes. High-stakes raids. Always successful, the force is rarely identified or wears a national uniform." Hawk paused, the lighter clicked, the distant puffs relit the cigar. "Recently there've been whispers that they've been hired for an attack that could destroy our prestige, even our interests, in the Third World."

Carter heard the cigar puffing, could almost smell the rank smoke.

"The ones who jumped me in Ethiopia could have been mercenaries."

"My thought exactly," Hawk said. "Find them, N3. Find out why that CIA man was killed and who attacked you. The murdered CIA man was Paul Lyons. His cover was on the staff in the Paris main office of Carr et Frères, a French food company that does a lot of business in Africa and was involved in aid efforts. Your cover will be that you're CIA."

"Cover or bait," Carter said.

"You knew the job was dangerous when you took it, N3." Hawk's voice became a distant chuckle.

SIX

It was still raining, the Seine almost up to the bridges. Nick Carter lit a morning cigarette and lay in bed staring out the windows of his Latin Quarter apartment at the gray drizzling sky. He'd spent ten days shuffling papers, asking careful, discreet questions, searching the dead CIA man's desk, files, apartment. Nothing.

Almost nothing.

Leslie stirred beside him in the bed. She reached out in her sleep, caressed his thigh, her fingers probing. She smiled up at him.

"*Bon jour*, Nicky."

"Sorry, Leslie, but it's another rotten *jour*."

She laughed. "Paris in the rain. Gene Kelly to sing and dance, *oui*?"

"Why does London get the rap when Paris has the same rotten weather?"

"The English enjoy their miserable weather. We French pretend it does not exist." She kissed him and pressed herself against him in the big bed. "Let's pretend the office does not exist. Paris does not exist. The world does not exist. Only us. Only us and we will stay in this bed forever."

"A beautiful dream," Carter said, "but we have to eat, pay the rent, indulge our habits."

Those were not his real reasons, but Leslie was not one of those who knew what he really did, so he could not tell her that bed and food and booze were not enough for him. He needed the chase, the contest, action and risk, the hurricane in his face.

She sighed. "We must go to the office?"

"We must."

"But tonight?"

"Tonight we don't have to be in the office."

She smiled, and they got up, showered, dressed, and went out through the silent corridors that smelled of damp carpeting and cooking into the steady drizzle of Paris. Leslie led him along the narrow Rue St-Sulpice to her own favorite café, the Monaco. Outside the windows Paris went to work fortified by coffee and croissants. They watched the people streaming past, heads bent to the rain, collars up.

Later, on the Métro, they hung from the bars with the hordes of other officegoers. Ten days of this, playing his role for those who did not know, playing the other role of a CIA man for those who did know, his real self to no one but himself. Ten days of filling out papers, sifting and talking and searching, and so far nothing.

"Lunch?" she said as they walked through the rain up the broad Champs-Élysées.

"I'll call your section."

The office of Carr et Frères was in an old building off the Champs-Élysées. A rickety elevator that must have been there since Napoleon's time carried them up to the fourth floor. Carter took his seat at the old-fashioned desk and pretended to plunge into the paperwork of shipping food to a thousand African cities, most in former French colonies. Europe had lost its political power, but its economic hold still strangled.

Then he found it.

Buried deep among the papers of American wheat to Zaïre for ground nuts to go to Belgium was a one-line note: *Le Basque, Tangier, forty-eight cases surgical B.M., (26) 40.07.26., Martin.*

The six numbers looked like a telephone number. He looked it up. Reims. Dialed. A long ringing.

"Oui?"

"Martin."

"So? And where have you been the last two weeks, Lyons?"

English. The voice had switched to beautiful, precise, only faintly accented English as soon as the name was spoken.

"Lyons is dead. This is Meyer, CRA-5. Investigating. You have instructions."

The line went dead. Carter hung up and sat back in his desk chair. He had no doubt that he had struck pay dirt. The only question was how and when would they contact him, whoever they were. And someone would be watching him now. Could be already. He let his eyes search the large room with all its desks. Which one would it be? Or would it be none of them at all? Someone from outside. . . .

He called Leslie. "The Cheval Noir?"

"Mmmmmmmmmmmmmmm."

"Half an hour."

He went back to work on the invoices and lading bills. The important thing was to continue his exact routine. At precisely 12:30 he shut off his adding machine and headed for Leslie's section.

It was a good lunch. With wine. When he left, it would be sudden and without notice. No good-byes.

There were aspects of his work to which he would never become accustomed.

He worked all afternoon, for Carr et Frères and for AXE. Carr et Frères made a profit; AXE didn't. He found no more notes or clues as to what had sent the CIA agent to Ethiopia and his death. No one contacted him.

Carter decided to speed things up. He told Leslie he had to work late but would meet her later at the Café Monaco. She pouted but asked no questions. By 6:30 no one had come near him. He quit and left. Alone he walked to the Métro, rode to St-Germain-des-Prés, and walked up . . . .

"Table nine, Deux Magots, CRA-5."

The man passed him on the stairs up and vanished out into the street. Carter turned left for the Café Deux Magots. The man was not ahead of him. Carter saw no trace of his contact and walked on along the boulevard to the crowded Deux Magots on the corner. It was going-home time, and Parisian cafés were always crowded then—a quick glass of wine or three to end the workday.

The barman nodded to him.

"*Un vin rouge*," Carter ordered. "Table nine, which one?"

"That one." The barman nodded to a corner table against two walls and served Carter his glass of red wine.

Carter carried the wine to the table and sat down. The man seated alone lowered his newspaper. A tall, thin man with a narrow, arrogant face and almost colorless eyes.

"What happened to Lyons?"

"You've checked me out?"

"We checked. What help do you need?"

"Check yourself for me."

The man smiled. "Military intelligence, Roger Martin. Run me through your computer. Need handprint? Voice? Day code?"

"Day code'll do."

"Boche."

Carter left the table and walked around to a public telephone hung on the wall. He watched Martin. The arrogant man had picked up his paper again. There was no need to check. Real or not, Martin knew he would check out clean. As Anna Ivanovna had learned, no amount of checking sources and computers made up for being careful. Anything that could be checked could be faked.

Martin lowered the newspaper again as Carter returned.

"So. Lyons?"

Carter told him what had happened to the CIA man. Martin nodded.

"It's been two weeks, give or take a day," the French military intelligence man said, "since we saw him last here to when you saw him killed in Ethiopia."

"Your last contact was here in Paris?"

Martin nodded. "In that same seat you're in."

"How did he get to Africa?"

Martin shrugged. "We heard through Le Basque."

That was the name on the note in Lyons's drawer at Carr et Frères. Carter showed Martin the cryptic message. Martin nodded again.

"He must have traced missing cases of surgical equipment from one of your aid shipments to the black market in Tangier. Le Basque would be the man."

"The man for what?"

"To follow up on it."

"Who is Le Basque?"

"Old maquis fighter. After the war many in the underground found it difficult to settle down, eh? Part thief, part hero. Part gangster, part undercover agent. We use them when we need them, jail them when we don't—if we can catch them. Since the war they have lived under the smooth surface by their wits, skills, and knowledge."

"World War Two? Aren't they getting a little old?"

Martin shrugged again, the universal French gesture. "It is a life-style, as you would say, where age is no handicap and even proof of ability, eh? They have children, followers, too. They go on. They have only three rules: loyalty to freedom and the people, loyalty to each other, and loyalty to France. In that order."

"How do I find this Le Basque?"

Another shrug. "I will put out the word, and with luck he will contact us and we will set up a meeting. It could take some days." A smile. "I hope you are not too bored at your office work."

"Not too," Carter said.

"Ah, yes, the agreeable Leslie. You are quick, CRA-5."

"When in France, right?" Carter smiled.

Martin was not amused. He folded his newspaper and stood up. "I will be in touch."

"Leslie is nice," Carter said, "but the trail is getting cold."

Martin shrugged. "As fast as is possible."

Alone, Carter finished his wine and considered his next move. Leslie was indeed lovely, but Tangier might prove more useful. Time was passing, yet he had other ways to find the Tangier black market. Maybe one more night. . . .

The gun pressed low into his back at the exact base of

his spine. The voice spoke quietly. In English.

"We walk out the small door beyond the rest rooms. Now."

Carter stood, drained his wine glass, set it down, then walked around his table and out the small side door.

And flung the door back against the man behind him.

"*Sacre . . . !*"

A cry of pain. The clatter of a gun.

Carter whirled, slamming into the man who was still staggering from being hit in the face, the gun somewhere on the cobblestones of the dark Parisian alley. The man kicked out. Carter twisted, took the kick on his thigh, and dropped the man with a single slash to the throat.

He got to the gun.

Three men came out of the shadows.

Carter swung the gun.

Someone kicked it away.

Hugo jumped into Carter's right hand. He plunged the stiletto into a faceless shadow in the dark alley and heard the scream. He kicked another shadow, slashed at the third, and ran for the distant light of the alley opening.

The opening closed.

Three more men stood against the light of the street, and Carter heard the scrambling behind him.

Wilhelmina slid into Carter's hand.

Three guns fired from the mouth of the alley.

Carter felt the blow in his chest and fell backward, blackness sliding over him.

SEVEN

Out of the black pit a light seemed to hang like a point light-years away, a star alone in a void. Carter did not open his eyes.

The pain pounded through his head. His mouth and throat gasped for water. Anything wet, cool. The pain of the pounding in his head screamed somewhere deep inside. The blow on his chest. Not a bullet, a drug dart. A tranquilizer gun usually used on animals. Drugged and taken, and his head pounded, pounded.

Carter made no sound. He concentrated behind closed eyes. Fought the violent headache. Thought. He was lying on his back. On something hard yet soft. His neck was supported on something hard yet also soft.

He heard distant sounds, movement. Someone walking. Metal striking metal and wood. Water. More than one person walking somewhere close, but not that close.

The pain surged through his head and he had to hold on.

He lay motionless.

His hands were on his chest. Not bound. His feet were not tied. Why?

A voice exclaimed in French. "*Alors*! His eyes flickered, Etienne!"

"He comes awake," another voice said in German.

A slow, thoughtful voice near him spoke in English. "He has been awake at least ten minutes, *mes amis*, perhaps longer. Fighting the headache and the dry throat. At least ten minutes, and he does not open his eyes, does not make a sound or move a muscle. Then tests his feet, hands. This one is not an amateur, *mes amis*, no. This one is to be reckoned with. Do you hear me, Monsieur Meyer, or whatever your real name is? You may open your eyes."

Carter said nothing. He remained motionless, his eyes closed. The deep voice laughed and continued to speak, now in French.

"No, not an amateur. The dagger up the sleeve, eh, Karl-Heinz? The karate blows, the Luger, the gas bomb on his leg. This man is the superagent, *non*?"

A surly German-accented French. "I saw the knife, he only winged me."

The deep voice was amused. "And you, Daniel? You tripped or that door would not have eaten your gun?"

"No," the voice that had spoken behind him in the Deux Magots said. "He is fast, very fast, a strong agent."

"You hear, Monsieur Meyer? CRA-5? They praise your skill, my men. We are friends. A small test in the alley. Come, you are among comrades."

Carter opened his eyes.

"Ah, welcome, Monsieur Meyer."

They were standing around him. He was in a small

living room, lying on a couch, his head against the arm. Through a lighted door there was a kitchen where two women were setting a table. A domestic scene.

Three old men, one as bald as an egg, were ranged around him. A fourth, the one with the deep voice, sat alone on a chair facing the couch. He had white hair and a drooping white mustache. He was at least seventy, probably older. A face of cordovan leather. Deep-set eyes lost among creases so hard they were like mountain ridges. Black eyes. Yellow teeth. A beret. A small man with a massive chest under a loose cotton shirt with an open neck and no collar, the chest thick and without wrinkles. Seventy-plus, with the eyes of ninety and the body of forty.

"Le Basque," Carter said.

The old man's eyes bored through Carter, through every inch, searched his hidden corners. He moved a thick, gnarled hand to dismiss the others.

"Leave us alone."

The other three old men left and closed the door. Le Basque went on studying Carter.

"Who killed Lyons?" he asked in English.

"You could have just called me on the telephone," Carter said.

"No," Le Basque said. "Ignorance is safety, *oui*?" The old man continued his scrutiny. "We did not expect such fierceness. The CIA are not usually a brigade alone."

"Sorry."

"No fatalities." The old man studied him. "So, the stiletto, the bomb, the ways with the women, eh? Who? Not CIA, no. Lyons was a child compared to you. I ask myself, who can this extraordinary person be? Military intelligence? Secret service? Special for the President of the United States? No, more powerful. A whisper comes—the Killmaster himself?"

The old man smiled. "But I do not ask, eh? Not a word. Nick Carter wishes to be Meyer, not a word, *oui*? Who else is not CIA but has a CIA number? Deeper than CIA . . . AXE even. An old name, long ago, very secret. Hawk? David? The war. The OSS? But what does an old man know? Not one word, eh?"

It was Carter's turn to study the old man. An innocent former resistance fighter, or something else? Guessing or testing? The old man had said enough to be checked; he had to know that. Or was he playing for an advantage, a lowering of Carter's defenses, before the check could be made? A one-time play, but perhaps worth it.

"I've heard of this Killmaster," Carter said. "You flatter me. I'm just a plain CIA agent, I'm afraid."

Le Basque shrugged the Gallic shrug. "As you wish, Nick. May I call you Nick? Later, you can ask Hawk, eh?"

"Yes, Hawk, the head of something called AXE, you said? A rumor, nothing more. I'd know if it existed."

Le Basque smiled. "Very well, to business. They have killed Lyons in Ethiopia?"

Carter described the scene he had witnessed. Le Basque listened intently. When Carter finished, the old man thought for a time, then nodded.

"So, the problem is how did he get to Ethiopia, eh? And why."

Carter watched him.

"You know what Lyons was working on?"

The shrug. "He was discreet, eh? But it is the black market of Tangier he wishes to be taken to. He is

American. He looks for cases of medical supplies, instruments. After Tangier we do not see him, but the American CIA is not investigating the Tangier black market, yes? It is the medical cases, the American supplies that—*voilà!*—vanish."

"That's the last place you saw him? In Tangier?"

Le Basque nodded.

"Can you take me?"

"Of course. When?"

"Now."

Le Basque smiled again. "Before you have checked me out?"

This time Carter shrugged. "As long as you take me where I want to go, I don't care what side you're on. I'll watch you."

The old man shook his head. "Such confidence for a plain CIA agent."

"Do we go?"

"Soon. First, we eat."

He stood up and opened the door into the kitchen. The three men and two women were already seated at the long table as if in some country kitchen in a provincial farmhouse. One of the women was as white-haired as Le Basque. The other wasn't.

"My wife Marie," Le Basque introduced, "and my daughter Chantal. These old bandits are Daniel with the very little hair, Raymond with the scar, and Karl-Heinz the Boche. Eat."

Chantal was taller than her father and almost as dark. She looked as if she had spent as much time in the sun as he had. She had jet-black hair and was slender but not too slender. Full breasts swelled a thin white blouse, firm hips curved the tailored wine-colored slacks. She nodded to Carter without interest, serving some kind of stew that smelled better than any restaurant Carter had been in for a long time.

He sat down and realized how hungry he was. He hadn't eaten since the lunch with Leslie. They all ate in silence, enjoying the meal without the tension of business or suspicion. These were men of experience. After the last bite, Carter excused himself and asked for the toilet. Behind the closed door he took out a small machine—hidden in a pack of cigarettes—that looked like a tiny tape recorder.

He balanced the instrument on his thigh as he sat, punched the "play" button, and adjusted the earpiece. The machine, powered by mini-batteries, was tied into AXE's worldwide computer through a special radio-telephone hookup relayed off satellites.

"Yes, N3," the sultry voice of the computer said.

"Background check, Le Basque, former French maquis."

There was a silence, then beeps and clicks. Then the sexy voice made its breathless report: "Le Basque, born Etienne Borotra, Cegama, Spain. Family immigrated to France. Fought in Spanish Civil War, World War Two underground resistance, Algeria. Since World War Two has worked for French military intelligence and operated black market and smuggling operations. One daughter, Chantal, reputed to be assistant to father."

"Relation to David Hawk, AXE."

Click, ping, squawk. "Unable to compute. Top-secret need-to-know only."

That was the damned trouble with machines no matter how sophisticated. It did not automatically translate "N3" into "Killmaster."

"Code Killmaster, compute need-to-know."

Click, ping, squawk. "Director Only. Cannot—"

The brusque voice of David Hawk broke in. "What the hell do you want with Director-Only data, N3, and where the devil are you? It's been ten days!"

"I'm sitting on the pot somewhere in Paris after making contact with French military intelligence and some ancient bandit named Le Basque who claims to be a personal acquaintance and old comrade-in-arms of yours. Know him?"

There was a cigar-chewing silence. "I know him."

"He pretends to know all about me. Do I believe him?"

"Believe him."

"Do I trust him?"

"With your life, yes. With your watch, no."

"Is there anyone from World War Two you don't know?"

"A few obscure Hungarians. Is that all you have to report, N3?"

Carter told him about the cryptic note in Lyons's desk, and his conversation with Martin of French military intelligence. "So it looks like Le Basque will be taking me to Tangier."

"Make it fast, N3. More aid has vanished, and I smell big trouble brewing," Hawk growled. "And say hello to that old rogue."

Carter punched off, stood, slipped the tiny machine into the cigarette pack in his pocket, and left the toilet. In the kitchen they were all having coffee and cognac.

"One before we go to work," Le Basque said, cocking his head at Carter. "Did I check, CRA-5?"

Carter drank the thick black coffee but skipped the cognac. It would be a long, hard trip however they went, and he didn't want his watch stolen.

"Hawk says hello," he said.

Le Basque laughed. "Ah, a small change of our lives here, there, and he would be the bandit, I the spy director with the bad stomach, eh? For me, I need the free life, the—how do you Americans say—'blowing on the wind.' "

Carter nodded, and his head seemed to explode. Grow larger and larger. The coffee! Hawk . . . confirmed . . . . The room . . . expanded . . . Hawk . . . wrong . . . mind was . . . fogged . . . faded . . . gone . . . .

He floated. Rocked. A baby in a cradle. On the treetop. Headache, but gentle now as he floated free in the rocking motion. He opened his eyes this time.

"You don't take any chances."

Chantal Borotra sat against a shadowy bulkhead and faced him in the dim light. "We cannot allow our locations to be known, not even to the Killmaster. Le Basque says everyone has a price, a weakness, a breaking point. It is how he has survived so well so long."

The black-haired woman was seated on a burlap-wrapped bundle in a row of other bundles in the narrow interior of what had to be an old C-47 transport that rocked and floated in slow flight. The old aircraft chugged along like some prehistoric bird. Ahead, between the bales and the cockpit, shadowy figures sat in a row like World War II paratroopers waiting for the drop.

"Is that how you survive, too? No chances?"

Her teeth flashed a brief white in the dim light of the transport interior.

"I listen to my father, and stay away from Killmasters."

Carter smiled at the girl's vague shape. There was something very self-contained about Chantal, and he had the feeling she was older than she looked. He filed this for future reference and continued to study the narrow interior of the old aircraft.

His eyes had grown accustomed to the dim light now, and he saw the guns. Mounted fore and aft, they were on both sides of the C-47, and aimed downward through large openings, they had a wide sweep of fire. Fifty-caliber machine guns, cannon, and rocket launchers. Viet Nam as well as World War II, transport and gunship.

"Where did you get this thing?" Carter asked.

Chantal looked around the crammed interior of the chugging aircraft. "A museum piece, *non*? The hero of World War Two, my father says. Without it there would have been no resistance. No supplies, no resistance."

"The guns aren't so museum. Puff the Magic Dragon damn near won us an unwinnable war."

Chantal nodded. "A very useful idea, my father says."

"You haven't said where you got it."

She smiled again. "As I said, a museum piece. Le Basque operates a World War Two museum, and this is an exhibit. We fly it all over France, Algeria, our old colonies. Old men and their toys, Le Basque says." She laughed. "Without the guns, of course."

"Where do they go in?"

She shook her head. "That you do not need to know."

"And the bales?"

She shrugged. "Patriotism costs money."

"Marijuana?"

"Call it our cash crop."

A gunship. Smuggling. Contacts all across Africa.

Whatever else they did, Le Basque and his group were self-sufficient. Marijuana and patriotic work with military intelligence and what else?

Carter shifted and looked out a window. Not far below, something shined black and silvery. A long shining path rippled to the distant moon. The old plane skimmed low over water.

"Where are we?"

Chantal looked at her watch. "We land outside Tangier in fifteen minutes. With luck."

"And without luck?"

The woman only shrugged again. A certain fatalism is necessary in any kind of war.

Fifteen minutes later the lumbering old aircraft began to descend.

Le Basque appeared in the cockpit door. "Hold on to what you can."

Below there was still water shining black and then the darker land without reflection or lights. Carter saw the narrow snake of a white road. Trees and mountains loomed straight ahead as the gray paleness of dawn touched the dry peaks. Then they were down, bouncing, yawing along the unlighted runway. A light appeared ahead, a point of light that waved left and left, and the old plane turned and finally shuddered to a stop.

Le Basque slid open the side door. "*Hola*, Ahoub, all quiet?"

"Of course, you old fool," the half-seen man behind the large flashlight said. "Another good landing, eh? You have the merchandise?"

"You have the money and the cars?"

"Ali!" the welcomer called through the graying dawn.

Instantly the headlights of six vehicles illuminated the tall, dark man in a flowing white burnoose.

Le Basque laughed and jumped down. "Good."

"Three for you, three for me," the man in the burnoose, Ahoub, said. "Gabouri says—"

Carter sensed rather than saw the movement beyond the glare of the twelve headlights.

"Down!" he shouted, and ran for the cockpit.

The hail of fire erupted like a volcano from behind the lights, shattering windshields, metal, windows. Ahoub screamed as his white burnoose turned red in an instant and his head exploded. The dead man was flung forward against Le Basque, showering the old man in blood, splattering the plane that had already begun to move.

Chantal leaped from the plane and ran to her father. The old maquis with the scar, Raymond, jumped out after her.

In the cockpit, Carter revved up the ancient plane, and lurched slewing and weaving down the runway. Bullets ripped through and around the rolling craft from the automatic weapons of whoever was hidden in the dawn light beyond the six vehicles.

"Open the guns!" the AXE agent shouted back through the cockpit door.

The bald old maquis, Daniel, shouted in French, "The guns! Stations!"

Carter straightened out the plane and, praying there was nothing hidden in the dawn, yanked it up off the makeshift airstrip and into a sharp left bank. He hoped the ancient craft had the power. It did. Carter smiled. They never made them any better than the old C-47.

He straightened out and lumbered back over the

airstrip in the slowly yellowing dawn, coming in low, barely above the long, low buildings and the six vehicles.

"Fire!" the bullet-headed Daniel shouted almost happily. "Fire! Fire everything!"

The gunship sprayed devastating fire into the gullies, bushes, trees, and hills that surrounded the makeshift airfield, and into the low wooden buildings.

Carter saw them in the lightening dawn: twenty or thirty men in gray fatigue uniforms armed to the teeth. The gunship blasted them out of their cover and holes, out of the bushes, from behind the buildings and the trees. They were not prepared for an attack from the air, or for the firepower of the old gunship. They broke and ran, panicked, to four trucks hidden off the main road to the west.

Like ants they scattered and ran and clambered into the vehicles. Heavy machine guns opened up on the gunship. Carter overshot, banked, and lumbered back. One of the trucks exploded in a sheet of flame. Then the old C-47 was past, and the trucks were on their way in retreat.

"Well done, my little cabbages!" Daniel cried to the old maquis behind the guns. "Again, American! After them!"

Carter shook his head. "They won't be back. We've got more urgent business on the ground."

He turned in a steep bank above the treetops and the barren desert ground littered now with the corpses of the attackers, and brought the old plane down quickly. He jumped out and ran to where Chantal knelt beside the shattered body of Ahoub and the fallen Le Basque. The scarred maquis, Raymond, lay dead behind them, his left arm shot away, half his head gone.

"Is Le Basque—?" Carter began.

Le Basque smiled and sat up. "Not a scratch. He saved me."

The old resistance fighter nodded to the shattered body of Ahoub in its bloody burnoose.

"Fell on me," Le Basque said in a kind of wonder. "Took everything that would have hit me. Who were they, Nick?"

"You tell me," Carter said. "This is your airstrip."

"No," Chantal said. "We use a different strip each time. There are hundreds around here. From the wars, the smuggling, the revolts." She held a piece of the dead Ahoub's burnoose against a flesh wound on her left side under her breast.

"And our enemies do not command such firepower, Killmaster," Le Basque said. "These, I think, were for you."

Daniel and the other old maquis were moving cautiously through the sprawled and mangled bodies of the attackers. Carter and Le Basque joined them. There were some fifteen dead, but no wounded.

"They took their wounded," Le Basque said. "A good unit."

"Yes," Carter said, but he was staring at the corpses. The gray field uniforms were exactly the same as the uniforms of the men who had attacked him in Ethiopia. Fifteen dead men in the same gray uniforms. Fifteen black men.

"Colonials," Le Basque noted. "See those cicatrice tattoos? Congo tribes."

"Not all," Carter said.

He kneeled down over three of the dead blacks whose bloody uniforms showed they had rank. They were lighter skinned, and their gaping mouths showed sophisticated dental work. They wore rings, not amulets. He searched their pockets and found their wallets.

"Americans," the Killmaster said.

Daniel bent over two more lighter-skinned bodies. The faces had bandit mustaches and Indian features. "Cubans?"

Carter stood up. "Mercenaries."

"For you," Le Basque said.

"Yes. But how did they know I was here?"

He looked around at the old resistance fighters and at Chantal, then at the bloody corpses sprawled across the silent airstrip. Daniel held up a crumpled envelope.

"Breast pocket." He nodded to one of the dead Cubans.

"What is it?" Carter asked.

Le Basque opened it and read the letter inside. He looked at Carter. "It's a kind of bill of sale: twenty cases to be picked up at a warehouse tonight, and it's signed Abad Al-Makdi."

Le Basque put the letter in his pocket. "We had better go and talk to my people."

"Who is Abad Al-Makdi?"

"The biggest international black market dealer in Tangier."

EIGHT

Water dripped somewhere, a slow, steady drip that echoed through the ancient catacomblike stone chamber. It could be noon out in the city, but there it was always midnight, only two bare bulbs to dispel the chill and gloom of the subterranean arches and corridors. Rats scurried outside the small circles of light, and the odor of wet earth and stone mixed with the faint stench of sewage.

"You have no idea who they were, Etienne?" one of the four old men behind the table asked Le Basque.

They were ranged like some secret tribunal at the scarred and worn table, old maquis, with others all around the dim stone chamber against walls, seated on tilted chairs. Le Basque, Chantal, and Carter sat together at a smaller table, cups of thick coffee in front of them.

"None. We think they were after the American here, Mr. Nicholas Meyer"—Le Basque smiled—"as he calls himself, eh?"

Every eye in the dank, shadowy chamber looked at Carter. The four leaders at the table studied him, hard-eyed.

"And who is this Mr. Meyer that you bring him here and bring, perhaps, danger to us?" another of the four said.

Le Basque told them about the CIA and the dead Lyons and Carter's mission. "Lyons was seen last here with us. Now Meyer follows his trail. We helped Lyons for French military intelligence—can we do less now?"

"What help does the American want?" one of the old maquis at the table asked.

"What can you tell me about a force of elite mercenaries supposed to be operating somewhere in Africa?"

The four looked at each other.

"We have heard rumors. For many years. We have asked questions; there are no answers. If it exists, it is well-hidden and well protected."

"And the international black market?"

The four looked toward the shadows of a stone arch. Someone moved, then came out into the light—a small, slender man in Western dress with a dark, cold, Arab face. He sat on a narrow chair, crossed his legs, and lit a thin, dark cigar.

"What do you wish to know about the black market, Monsieur Meyer?" His English was heavily accented, and it wasn't a French accent. It was Arabic or Berber.

"Has there been a lot of merchandise turning up with U.S. Aid markings on it?"

The slender man smoked his thin cigar. "Yes."

"Do you know where it comes from?"

"Everywhere. From all the countries where your aid is sent."

"Any specific people? Names?"

The man almost smiled. "No, Monsieur Meyer. No names."

"And where is it all going?"

"That we do not know for sure." The dark face was immobile, the hawk nose and hooded black eyes turned toward Carter. "There is some evidence it goes all to a single destination. But it is a guess, a hint, no more."

Carter looked at the four old maquis behind the table. "Does he know what he's talking about?"

"He knows," one said.

"Walid Daba operates in the black market," another said.

"And is chief of detectives of the police."

Carter looked at the slender, hawk-faced man. The man smiled now. "Orderly crime is better than disorderly, Monsieur Meyer, and who can keep order better than one who is on both sides?"

"That attack this morning wasn't so orderly," the Killmaster said.

"They did not come from my territory," the thin police detective said.

"Where did they come from?"

A shrug. "That is not my job."

"Anyone?" Carter said to the four old men at the table.

"We have asked all our people in Africa," one of them said. "We get no answers."

"Do you have any answer to how they knew I was landing with Le Basque at that airstrip?"

No one spoke in the dim, dank stone chamber with its two bare bulbs and dripping water, rats singing somewhere in the shadows, the city above close yet distant.

"It had to be someone among you," Carter said.

"No," Le Basque said. "None of mine."

"French intelligence, then," Carter said.

"No," Chantal said. "Your own people, CIA man?"

"I doubt it."

"Someone you met in Paris?" one of the old men said. "At Carr et Frères?"

"No one broke my cover." Of that Carter was sure. Or was he? Leslie?

"You are so sure, American?" the thin police detective, Walid Daba, asked.

"As sure as any of you about your friends," Carter said.

"We are sure. We have all served too long together not to know," Le Basque said.

In the silence of the underground chamber the thin policeman cleaned his fingernails with a small knife.

"The attackers had a contact with this Al-Makti," Carter said. "How do we talk to him?"

"*You* do not," Le Basque said. "*We* will find him, talk to him."

Carter shook his head. "My job. No other way."

"He never leaves the Casbah," one of the old maquis at the table said. "There is no way for you to go in there."

"He comes out," Carter said, "or I go in."

Le Basque turned to Walid Daba. "Can you do it some way?"

The dark man studied Carter with his heavy-lidded eyes. "Perhaps I can do something." He stood up. "Come, American." He nodded to Le Basque. "We will be ready at sundown."

The sun had just gone down behind the Great Mosque when the three men met at the southwestern gate of the Medina. Le Basque was there first, coming out of the shadows of the early night street with its crowds of turbaned and fezzed and robed people mixed with those in Western dress. He nodded to the slender police detective; Walid Daba stared at Carter.

"Is it the American?"

Carter rolled his eyes, shook his head, and pointed to his face. He wore a blackish, indigo-dyed turban and desert veil, and a dirty white burnoose, only his eyes showing. Brass plates with Arabic script were on the turban. Walid Daba nodded.

"He speaks Arabic, but with the wrong accent for this area, and he does not speak Berber. So he is a deaf and dumb Tuareg from the desert I have befriended."

"Could he pass to a Tuareg?"

"We won't meet any," the Berber detective said, "or, with luck, anyone who knows a real Tuareg."

They went through the gate and up the ancient hill to the old Sultan's Palace and the walled Casbah, moving slowly through the dark, narrow streets that were little more than passages between the old stone walls of the buildings with their narrow windows or no windows at all. They passed dim cafés where silent robed figures drank their mint tea. Few people moved along the narrow passages, yet noise came from everywhere: radios, television sets, drums, flutes, angry voices and the singing of women, the barking of dogs and scurrying of feet, human and rodent. A cacaphony from somewhere just beyond the shadows.

"There," Walid Daba said softly.

Among the old walls, they were across a small open square from a café where a throng of Moroccan people sat drinking, smoking, and talking, animated but not loud.

"It's Abad Al-Makdi's headquarters. The large building to the right is his warehouse. The four men seated at the front table inside the door where they can watch the warehouse entrance are Al-Makdi's guards. The dog himself is that ancient relic in the blue robes and the fez at the rear table.''

Carter studied the café across the square from above his veil. The four guards looked bored and indolent. Judging by their heavy eyes and well-filled robes, they hadn't seen action in a long time. Al-Makdi himself had to be close to eighty, as thin and dried as a walking mummy, a wizened monkey face under an oversize fez, rich blue robes hanging as if from a skeleton. Alone, he drank only Perrier, his nervous eyes watching everything and nothing, his emaciated fingers moving in spasms of trembling as if unconnected to the brain under the fez.

"Here comes his business," Walid Daba whispered where they were hidden in the shadows across the small square.

Three men in business suits, tall and short, dark-skinned and light, each bold and furtive and nervous all at the same time, came out of the windowless old medieval warehouse building and across the square to the café. One of the fat guards patted them down in good Hollywood style, looking like someone out of the movie *Casablanca* and knowing it, and waved them to the table where Al-Makdi sat.

"They'll haggle for hours," Walid Daba said wearily.

"I want to get into that warehouse," Carter said from behind his veil. "One of you can watch him."

"No need," Walid Daba said. "He won't move from there for at least an hour, probably two. It's the only fun he has nowadays. Come."

The slender detective slipped through the darkness of the narrow passages past the windowless three-story building. An even narrower alley ran along the rear of the monolithic building. A low grating was set into the base of the rear wall. Daba kneeled down and pulled at the grating. Nothing happened. The detective swore.

Carter crouched and pulled the rusty iron grate out.

He dropped down into the darkness. Daba and Le Basque came behind him as silent as cats. Daba shined a thin light. They were in a cramped stone window-well with a wooden panel on the inner wall. Daba took out a key, opened the lock on the panel, and swung it in. Carter went in first.

There was another drop, and then he stood on the stone floor of a long, low room with muted indirect lighting, rows of stacked crates, boxes, and containers; neat and precise, cool and soundless. The three of them walked slowly along the rows, their footfalls muted, a layer of sweat on Carter's neck under the stifling veil and burnoose.

"Soundproofed and air-conditioned," he said.

"Naturally," Le Basque said. "An old Arab but a modern black marketeer, eh? The merchandise is valuable."

They moved down the rows. Carter examined the crates and boxes and cartons. There were medicines intended for Zaïre, farm implements for Mali and Rwanda, pumps and generators for Zambia, rows and rows of foodstuffs for Sudan and Chad, Mali and Mauritania. All marked with the stamps of U.S. Aid, and U.N. Relief Aid, and Red Cross International Relief.

"Why hasn't he moved them out?" Carter wondered.

"A good question," Walid Daba said. "There would be no problem selling all this tomorrow in half the countries of the world."

"Maybe Al-Makdi has an agreement," Le Basque said.

Daba nodded, thoughtful. "A single buyer is even more profitable, yes. Less overhead, transport, protection."

"Where's his office?" Carter asked.

"Upstairs," Daba said.

They moved quickly along the rows of boxes and crates through the silence and the faint hum of the air conditioning.

Ancient, rickety wooden stairs led upward. Walid Daba took out a 9mm Beretta. Le Basque had his Uzi submachine gun. Carter held Wilhelmina under his robes.

They went up.

At the top Walid Daba used his keys on a locked door. They stepped out into another large room the length of the ancient building. It too was dimly lighted and filled with boxes and crates, but here there was no soundproofing, no air conditioning, and the ancient stones gave off their odor of dust and mold that had been here since Carthage ruled the Mediterranean.

"Goods for local sale in the bazaars, markets," Walid Daba said. "Not such elegant treatment as the booty below, eh?"

"Where's the office?" Carter searched the gloomy old shadows over his veil.

The chief of detectives led them back to an arched section that must have seen dancers and slave girls in the days when Roman legions marched the narrow streets outside. It was now glassed in and had the odor of Victorian wood, the furniture from the days of the East India Company: old wooden desks and filing cabinets, rattan chairs, overhead a punkah waiting for someone to pull it by its long cord and fan the room. Walid Daba pointed to the filing cabinets.

"I'll take the main desk, you take—"

The man came through a door at the rear of the old office. An old man carrying a bucket and mop.

Walid Daba whirled.

"Silence!" he hissed in Arabic.

The old man froze, stared, terror on his wrinkled face. Daba smiled.

"Be calm, old man."

Carter saw his hand. The old man's face was a mask of terror. He trembled, cringed, and held to the wall with his free hand.

"His hand!" Carter said.

The old man tried to run. Where his hand had held to the wall, there was a small electric button.

Daba shot the old man in the head.

"*Merde*," Daba said softly, then turned to face the front door.

Walid Daba shot the first one through the front door: a fat man whose dirty gray burnoose spouted red where the Beretta tore a hole in his heart.

Wilhelmina sent the second screaming backward holding the black hole between his eyes.

Le Basque faced the other way, his Uzi cutting down the two men who came through the rear door.

One staggered blindly into a wall, then sprawled backward through the door. The other got off a shot. Walid Daba cursed and held his left arm. Le Basque finished off the man who had shot, stitching red across his white burnoose.

"Now!" Carter ran for the front door.

Le Basque raced after Carter.

They burst out the front door of the ancient warehouse into the night of the small square with Daba and his bloody arm behind them. Three gray-robed men blocked the square. Le Basque's Uzi cut down two; Hugo jumped into Carter's hand and was hurled into the throat of the third guard. Walid Daba went past them.

The small square was silent. Carter retrieved Hugo

and followed Le Basque into the café where no one sat now—except Al-Makdi and Walid Daba. The café was empty, as was the square; Al-Makdi sat at his table in his blue robes with Daba's Beretta at his head.

"The lower warehouse, worthless pig," Daba said. "Where does it all go?"

Al-Makdi's eyes rolled in his dried leather face. Daba cocked the Beretta.

"One second, garbage."

"Russians," Al-Makdi said.

"All of it?" Carter said as he and Le Basque stood at the table in the empty café.

Al-Makdi nodded.

"In return for what?"

Al-Makdi's eyes bulged, searched for help, escape. Walid Daba shot him in the arm. The old man screamed as his bone smashed and blood splattered across the floor and table.

"For what?" Carter said.

"Boxes," the old man gasped. "Wood boxes, heavy."

"Boxes of what?"

"Don't know."

Daba shot at the old man's foot. He missed. The old man screamed.

"They take them! I never see!"

"Who?"

The old man shivered with terror, shook his head, and babbled. "Mamba. Pay, take, no names. Bring merchandise for Russia, pay me, take boxes. No questions."

"They bring all the Aid material? American?"

The old man nodded, his eyes wide.

"Where from?"

"Zaïre."

"What do they—"

The old man's eyes jumped out of his head. Two men stood in the café doorway, their dark faces contorted with hatred. One of the men was the guard shot by Le Basque in the warehouse, an arm dangling dead, dripping blood. The other was an older man whose eyes bored into Al-Makdi.

"Dog! Pig!" they shouted in Arabic.

Le Basque and Carter fired. Both men fell backward, but two bombs flew across the room.

Carter went out a window. Le Basque fell on top of him. The café exploded. Glass and wood and metal and flesh and blood showered the square.

Carter and Le Basque jumped up.

The two men who had thrown the bombs lay dead in the square.

Inside the shattered café the legless body of Al-Makdi raised one stump of an arm and stared at Carter and Le Basque as the blood poured from his leg arteries and life drained from his amazed eyes.

Walid Daba's headless body lay across the splintered table, the Beretta still in his hand.

Carter turned and vanished into the Casbah. Le Basque followed him into the night.

NINE

David Hawk's gruff voice was low under the roar of the old C-47's engines. "I don't like the sound of it, N3. Something's gearing up to happen."

"If they are the mercenary group you're worried about," Carter said into his miniaturized transmitter, "they're operating everywhere we send aid in Africa."

"With the Soviets behind them, or just using them to discredit us, or worse."

"Unless they're using the Russians," Carter said.

There was a long silence at the other end of the secret radio-satellite connection.

"For what?" Hawk said.

"Yeah," Carter said. "That's what I have to find out, isn't it?"

Hawk chewed his cigar in the distant Washington headquarters of AXE. "Find out fast, N3. Those boxes make me very nervous."

"We'll be landing in Kinshasa in an hour," Carter said.

"Keep in touch," Hawk growled. "And I mean close

touch, N3. I've got a strong feeling that when this one goes up we'll have to move fast."

The instrument went silent. Carter sat there in the dim belly of the C-47. In the lumbering aircraft, Le Basque was again up in the cockpit piloting, Chantal with him this time. Four other vigorous old maquis sat dozing in the dim light with Carter. Below, the desert had changed to jungle, and winding dirt tracks, and rivers snaking through the thick vegetation.

Le Basque came back from the cockpit. The old man sat beside Carter, stretched out his legs with a sigh, and lit a joint. The acrid marijuana smoke filled the cabin.

"Who's flying this thing?" Carter asked.

"Chantal, eh? Fine pilot, taught her myself." Le Basque grinned. "So. You have talked to my old friend?"

"Exactly where are we going, old man?"

Le Basque laughed. "Very well, business it is, eh? So, we are in luck. My old underground commandant, Julien Sorel, retired to Zaïre many years ago and opened a hotel outside Leopoldville—now called Kinshasa. We were able to contact him, and he will meet us at his hotel. He knows of no mercenary force of the magnitude you suspect, but he thinks he or his contacts in the Zaïre government may be able to give us some leads."

"What kind of leads?"

Le Basque carefully pinched out his joint, slipped it into the breast pocket of his camouflage fatigues, stood up, and turned toward the cockpit. "To where some American aid for Zaïre disappeared."

The old man walked back through the dim belly of the vintage aircraft to the pilot's cabin, and Carter sat in the dark and thought about the disappearance of American aid in Zaïre and everywhere else. Hawk had said that people were already becoming ugly about failed American promises, American lies, American schemes. The U.S. could lose Africa, and what else? What was in the boxes from the USSR, and who were the soldiers in gray?

Carter became aware of the broad Congo River below and the widening into the lakelike Stanley Pool with the neat white buildings of Brazzaville on the right bank below the Pool and the tall buildings and green expanses of Kinshasa on the left bank. The old transport lumbered in low across the great river toward the high sandy plateaus behind Kinshasa and began its descent into the airport of the capital of Zaïre.

Chantal came back as they taxied to an empty area of the field.

"We've got a welcoming committee," she said quickly. "Americans aren't too popular here, especially CIA men. Is your French good enough to be my husband?"

"My French and everything else," Carter said, grinning.

"Keep your mind on your work, monsieur. You may need it," she said. "Here is your passport. You are Albert Chénier, an engineer of roads and cities. Your picture is already in place, a precaution."

Carter took the passport. It was French, proclaimed him to be everything she had said, and someone had taken his picture with a Polaroid camera and pasted it in with the proper seals. Le Basque and his people believed in being prepared.

"Who is the real Albert Chénier?"

"My husband," Chantal said and turned away. "He is dead."

Carter had no time to question Chantal further. The C-47 door burst open, and a violent voice shouted in bad French, "Out! Immediately! Everyone! Now!"

Outside the window Carter saw what looked like a full company of black soldiers, all spit and polish, white leggings and red berets. Armed to the teeth, they ringed the C-47, bayonets fixed and rifles aimed. Two ramrod noncoms stood below the open door shouting and gesticulating furiously for everyone to descend from the plane.

Le Basque was out first. He strode to the NCOs just as ramrod and just as furious and just as violent and in a lot better French.

"Imbecile! Idiot! Do you know whom you are threatening?"

The old man stood nose to nose with one of the noncoms. The rest of the old maquis jumped down behind him. Chantal and Carter came last.

"Wait until General Mobutu hears how you greeted Le Basque when he came to Zaïre!"

The noncoms looked uncertain and retreated a step. There was a stir in the ranks of the soldiers surrounding the old C-47, and a tall, elegant major came slowly through the soldiers and up to the group. He carried an ebony swagger stick and touched Le Basque on the chest with it.

"You are a smuggler, old man," he said in much better French. "We have been informed. We will now search your aircraft."

Le Basque nodded. "So. Who has played that old trick? Go ahead, Major, search."

The major held his swagger stick suspended, a small uncertainty at the edges of his arrogant eyes.

"Search the aircraft," he said to the noncoms.

The two NCOs barked their orders in a combination of some local native language Carter did not know and bad French. Soldiers swarmed up into the C-47.

"What will they find?" Carter whispered to Chantal.

"Nothing."

"You're sure?"

"Of course. We're not fools, monsieur. This kind of thing happens a great deal down here."

Le Basque paced angrily, glaring at the ranks of soldiers around the plane with their guns at the ready. The other old maquis stood in the shade of the aircraft out of the fierce equatorial sun.

"Sergeant!"

The major stood in the C-47 doorway. The senior NCO walked quickly to stand beneath the officer.

"Take them. Put cuffs on that old one with the big mouth."

The arrogant officer held out a large plastic bag, let a stream of white powder fall down into the dirt, and smiled at Le Basque.

"Someone set us up, Killmaster," Le Basque said. "We smuggled no heroin."

Carter, Le Basque, and the other four maquis sat on the stone floor of the military brig at an army barracks on the outskirts of Kinshasa. Chantal had been taken somewhere else over Le Basque's violent but useless protests. All the old leader had to show for it was a bruised cheek and sore ribs from rifle butts.

"Of course someone set us up," Carter growled, sounding almost like Hawk even to himself. "The question is who, and why? This time, no one around me except Hawk knew we were coming down here, and Hawk didn't know until we were on the transport. Who could've planted that heroin?''

Le Basque nodded. ''One of my own people; it must be. Unless . . . Walid Daba could have had a confederate—he could have passed on what Abad El-Makdi told us before they were killed.''

''He'd have to have done it in about one minute flat, while we were watching and he was hammering Al-Makdi.''

''We were watching Al-Makdi, Killmaster.''

''How did he transmit? A hidden mike in his Beretta?''

''I have seen things more unusual than that. But it would not have had to be in the gun. It would not even have to have been transmitted then. A small tape recorder in his pocket—a confederate knows about the aid all coming to Tangier from Zaïre.''

Carter watched the fierce old man. ''You don't want to face up to it, do you. One of your maquis? Maybe someone you've fought beside your whole life?''

Le Basque was silent. ''No, I do not want to face that.'' He looked at Carter in the stifling heat of the crowded cell. ''I do not want to, but I will. Who? I ask myself this. Who? Daniel? Karl-Heinz? Chantal?''

One of the other old maquis looked at the floor. ''She is not with us, Etienne.''

''No, she is not with us,'' Le Basque said.

Another of the old men said, ''Because she is a woman? A separate cell for a woman to show how civilized they have become?''

''That is possible,'' Le Basque said.

The others were silent, looking at the floor or up at the high, narrow barred windows that let in all the light and air in the room.

''We won't find out in here,'' Carter said. ''As soon

as it's dark, we go and find Chantal and some answers."

All the maquis stared at him.

"You have wings, American?" one said.

"Perhaps one of your 'Star Wars' weapons?"

"A wall disintegrator?"

"A transporter that will wisk our molecules through the stone?"

Le Basque rubbed his chin. "I suspect Monsieur Meyer has something up his sleeve, eh?"

Carter smiled. "When it's dark."

The old men hooted softly and went back to staring at the walls and floor and high barred windows. Carter lay back against the prison wall. Le Basque watched him.

"They took your weapons, your tiny communication instrument," the old maquis said.

"Yeah, I'll have to stop and get those back."

"Our weapons and aircraft too, eh?"

"Those too."

"Such confidence," Le Basque said. "Or such bravado."

"A little of both," Carter said.

He closed his eyes and waited for night. Le Basque lay down on the floor and slept. A lifetime of training teaches one to conserve energy while waiting for the time of action. Carter dozed, but he did not sleep, alert for any sound. It was a setup, yes, but who was the target, and who was doing the setting up? And why? Who would come to the cell first, the guards or the night?

He waited.

The night came first.

"Time," Carter siad.

None of them moved.

"Form a pyramid so I can climb up to the windows." The Killmaster took off his belt and extracted three pieces of his special AXE striated tape. "Now!"

"Now!" Le Basque echoed, jumping up. He motioned for Daniel and Karl-Heinz to link arms, and for the other two to stand on their shoulders.

Carter climbed onto the shoulders of the top two, quickly wrapped the tape around three of the iron bars, and scratched each with his fingernail. In seconds the bars had melted through. He removed each bar and sent it down hand to hand to the floor. From the heel of his shoe he took his escape wire mechanism, attached it to the stump of one iron bar, and lowered himself to the cell floor.

"I will go first," Le Basque decided.

"And I'll come last," Carter said.

Le Basque held the thin wire, activated the mechanism, and rose up to the window. He looked out warily, then slipped through the narrow opening and out, his hands holding to the stone windowsill and then vanishing.

Each of the maquis went up in turn, and out, and dropped to the ground in the night outside the walls. Carter was last. He went up to the window, retrieved the wire and mechanism, returned it to the heel of his shoe, slid through, and dropped lightly to the dark ground.

Hands grabbed him instantly.

Covered his mouth.

Held him in an iron grip.

TEN

Carter slammed a knee into the groin of one man. Pulled his arm free. Chopped the panting face of another. Kicked, broke his other arm free. Crouched, and . . .

Looked into the muzzle of an M-16 aimed at his eye.

"You will be very quiet!"

Carter froze, staring into the eyes of the old man behind the M-16. He saw three other old men around him, guns leveled, the two on the ground he had kicked and chopped down, and beyond them Le Basque smiling at him.

"Friends, Killmaster," Le Basque whispered.

Carter saw Daniel and Karl-Heinz and the other two old maquis in the dark night, standing apart and watching. He saw Chantal and maybe fifteen other gray-haired men all armed with M-16s. The man holding the rifle to his face spoke again.

"We are friends, eh? You see Le Basque? You see his daughter?"

Carter nodded and slowly straightened up. The man

lowered his rifle, but his eyes remained wary, alert. Le Basque laughed softly.

"I think, Degrange, you are fortunate that the American understood so quickly the situation, eh?"

The man with the rifle considered Carter. He was short and thick, with iron-gray hair and a squashed face like a lion or an old prizefighter, and a long scar from his left eye to his jawbone.

"So?" the man, Degrange, said. "You think I am not a match for this one, Borotra?"

"I think you are not," Le Basque said, smiling.

Degrange rubbed his jaw, continuing to assess the Killmaster. "Perhaps you are right. Still, if I were younger, well—"

"Does someone want to tell me what is going on here?" Carter asked.

"Chantal, explain as we march," Degrange snapped.

Le Basque, the four other old maquis who worked with him, and the armed strangers all fell into line and moved quickly off into the night. Chantal marched beside Carter.

"These are the men of my father's old commandant, Julien Sorel. They have immobilized the Zaïrean soldiers, rescued me, and recovered all our weapons. Now we escape."

"How did they know we were here?"

Ahead, Le Basque laughed. "Because, Killmaster, they put us here! A little ruse, to protect themselves and their organization from observation. I am not the only one who learns these things. This way, we are together, but no one can know we are with them, eh?"

"They planted that heroin? Set us up?"

"That way, no one sees us join, eh? No one knows where we are."

"No," Carter said, thoughtful, "no one knows. Did they rescue my weapons too?"

Degrange dropped back from the head of the fast-moving column as it slipped silently through the thick undergrowth in the night. "Of course, American."

He held out Wilhelmina, Hugo, and Pierre with all their accessories.

"Alas, the small tape recorder was destroyed in a slight scuffle with the Zaïrean major."

"Unfortunate," Carter said, watching the leonine face of Degrange under the thick gray hair. "Where are we going?"

"You will find out, American."

A road appeared, and trucks loomed ahead in the African night. Degrange urged them all into the three trucks, and they quickly drove off along the pale narrow track of the bush road. They seemed to go north around the glow of light in the dark sky that was Kinshasa itself. From time to time soldiers stopped them, but the strangers seemed to have the proper passes or papers and were allowed to go on. They turned west, Carter saw by the stars, and finally south again. The Killmaster caught glimpses of the broad shine of the great river itself.

Carter spoke quietly to Chantal. "Tell me about this Julian Sorel."

"Sorel? He is one of the legends of those days," the dark-haired woman said beside him in the dark, bouncing truck. "He was my father's commandant. He brought them all through, but after the war he could not find a place for himself in France. He could not settle again for the small job. So he came to the Congo and worked many years for the Belgian government, then opened a resort hotel here west of the city. It has become the most famous bar-hotel in Zaïre. They say there is nothing that happens in Africa that Monsieur Sorel does not know.''

One of the armed men grinned at them. ''That is true, Mademoiselle Chantal. The boss knows everything worth knowing. It is a fine life here, soft and easy, eh? You should all come and join us. It is time Le Basque and the others retired, settled down to some comfort as we have. And fighting, smuggling, spying is no work for a woman.''

The old freedom fighters began to talk among themselves, comparing their lives, the Zaïre people urging Le Basque's men to settle permanently as they had.

''Old men should rest, lie in the sun. We are all too old now.''

''Speak for yourself,'' someone said, laughing.

The others all began arguing as they rolled on around the city and then west along the banks of the broad river in the night, the moon a path of light along the surface of the water. Then the trucks suddenly stopped.

''We are here. Everyone out.''

The all jumped quietly from the trucks. Carter saw a high whitewashed stucco wall disappearing into thick jungle in both directions in the dark night. Beyond the wall the shadowy roofs and giant trees towered all around in the moonlight. A large sign hung over the closed iron gates: Hôtel du Croix de Lorraine, Julian Sorel, Prop. Degrange had his and Le Basque's old resistance fighters lined up, and the iron gate opened from inside.

''So,'' the smashed-face old maquis said. ''Welcome to Hôtel du Croix de Lorraine.''

They all went through and the gates closed behind them. Carter turned and noticed one of Degrange's armed men drop off and take up position at the gate. They moved on through lush grounds that opened onto a well-manicured lawn and an enormous three-story white hotel across the vast expanse of grass dim in the moonlight. Towers rose above the three stories, and all the roof area was a red slate that gave a rich contrast to the white of the giant frame building.

Inside, the lobby was broad and airy, polished bare floors with expensive Oriental area rugs and white rattan furniture, wide stairs up on both sides, a polished reception desk and an open arch into the restaurant that was almost as large as the lobby itself. Ranged in the center were white-and-blue-uniformed native hotel attendants.

"The staff will show you to your rooms," Degrange said. "We will serve dinner in an hour. You should all have time to shower and rest a little. Monsieur Sorel regrets he cannot be here tonight, but I will do my best to fill in for the commandant."

The large, rambling hotel appeared to be almost empty. There were few guests in the bar as Carter walked past behind his uniformed attendant. It looked as if each of them were being given a private room. Carter showered, shaved, and found his suitcase waiting in the room after he came out of the shower. He changed into a khaki safari suit, wiped the dust of the airport and cell from his boots, and went down to the dining room.

"Nick!" Le Basque called from a long table.

Carter threaded his way through the tables to Le Basque, Chantal, Daniel, Karl-Heinz, and the other two from Le Basque's Parisian unit. The room was packed with gray-haired, white-haired, and bald men, many wearing decorations on their worn fatigues and work clothes. It was more like a World War II reunion than just dinner. The only other time Carter had seen anything that resembled it was a reunion of a Waffen SS division some years ago in Germany. Old enemies tended to grow more like each other as the years passed.

But there were no speeches, and the dinner was too good for a reunion. When it was over, most of the old soldiers drifted away to their quarters somewhere out on the grounds. Degrange invited Le Basque and his party into the bar where they all sat on rattan couches around a small table.

"So, Borotra, it is unfortunate that the commandant cannot be here, but he told me to help you as much as I could. What brings you down here to the commandant?"

Le Basque told Degrange about the missing American aid material all over Africa, and the murder of the CIA man in Ethiopia. "So Monsieur, ah, Meyer has been sent to replace Lyons and finish the job."

Degrange looked at Carter. "You are CIA? Searching for your lost aid and cash?"

"That," Carter said, "and looking for information on a force of mercenaries who wear gray uniforms, go well armed, and seem to have a special interest in me and the aid material."

"Mercenaries?"

Carter nodded. "Well trained, well equipped, and apparently international." He told Degrange about the attack at the airfield outside Tangier.

"Well," Degrange said, looking from Carter to Le Basque and back. "Now, tell me what you are *really* doing here. Why do you want to contact Commandant Sorel? You are not a simple CIA man. No, much more. You think we do not have our contacts in the CIA, in the governments? In France? In Zaïre? One man, alone, sent to find an unknown force of mercenaries? Ridiculous, American. Unless that man is very special, eh? A superspy, perhaps? Killmaster, Le Basque has called you. Who are you?''

Le Basque protested. "A joke, Degrange. A name played with in jest.''

"Am I laughing, Borotra? You think I am a fool? We have heard of the so-very-secret Killmaster of the United States. You have heard too, eh? Either this American has fooled you, or you are lying to me! Perhaps you lie about everything? Mythical mercenaries! We have lived here now for forty years. We would know of such a force anywhere and we do not!''

They were suddenly aware of the other old maquis at the doors into the bar. Chantal stood up.

"You do not know what you are becoming involved in, Degrange," she said. "You are right. There is more to this than the theft of some American aid or a simple mercenary unit. We think these things are tied together, and to some plan that could destroy us all—tied to a code word: mamba.''

Degrange blinked at her. "Who is us, Mademoiselle Borotra?''

"The free world, Monsieur Degrange," Chantal said.

Degrange scowled. "You speak for the free world, then?''

"My employer and Monsieur Meyer's employer do— France and the United States of America.''

"So? Then you speak for France?''

"As much as military intelligence speaks for its country.''

A murmur ran through the old maquis watching at the doorways into the bar. Degrange looked at Le Basque and at Carter, then back at Chantal.

"You are French military intelligence, Mademoiselle Chantal?"

"You can check."

"Yes, I can. Marais! Bring the captain!"

Carter heard someone move out of the crowd and across the wooden floor and up the wide stairs. Then there was a silence in the bar ringed by the old maquis and the vast hotel itself. The only sounds were the distant laughter of some tourists at the pool, British voices in the smaller bar, a radio playing somewhere, and the distant cries of monkeys in the jungle. Le Basque and Carter sat watching Chantal. The Killmaster shifted slightly in his chair so that Hugo and Wilhelmina were ready. The figures at the door nearest the stairs moved, parted, and a tall, slender man in impeccable civilian clothes came in and nodded to Degrange.

"You wanted to see me, Degrange? It had better be important. I was—"

"It's important, Captain. Do you know that woman?"

The tall man looked at Chantal. Then he looked at Le Basque, the four others, and Carter. Then he nodded to Degrange. "Yes, I know her. A very dangerous enemy, the lady. I suggest we take them all to the cellar at once."

There was a stir among the watching maquis, a low growling of anger. Degrange motioned. Some hotel attendants appeared. They had rifles. Carter watched them. They seemed to know how to use the rifles, and they moved with a lot of assurance for bellboys and waiters.

"Take them down to the basement," Degrange ordered.

The armed attendants marched them through the

muttering maquis and across the polished wood of the lobby out into the African night. Outside they were taken around the hotel and down stone steps into the old stone basement under the building. Degrange and the tall man led them along dim passages past storerooms of food and wines to a small room crowded with electronic equipment.

"Tell your men to wait outside," the tall man ordered Degrange.

Degrange hesitated.

"Do it, Jacques, or Sorel will have your ass," the tall man said.

Degrange blinked, then spoke in some African language to the armed men. They went out and closed the door. The captain sat down and lit a cigarette.

"All right, Chantal, what the hell's going on?"

"I could ask you the same, Henri," Chantal said.

Degrange stared at them. "You said—"

"That she was a dangerous enemy," the tall man said. "She is, to the enemies of France. She is military intelligence, if that was what you wanted to know."

"Captain Baudou works in a different section, but we know each other," Chantal said. "What are you doing down here, Henri?"

"He is doing the same as you," Degrange growled. "That was why I got suspicious. We've been helping him track down that mercenary outfit no one can locate. No one else was supposed to know about them."

"You?" Henri Baudou said, looking at Le Basque and Carter. "The Americans too?"

Chantal told the military intelligence captain all that had happened so far, and why they had come to Zaïre.

"You think it's this gang of mercenaries stealing and

selling the U.S. aid? Dammit, that must be where they're getting the cash to buy their weapons. Those they don't steal.''

"How did you get assigned to find them?" Chantal asked.

Baudou sat and smoked. "For years now my section has been trying to locate them. All we have had is rumors, some bloody raids with no survivors, and no loud claims of responsibility made by any known groups. Swift attacks and vanishings. Gold stolen. Weapons, food, aid material. The only information we've found is a possible code name: Black Mamba.''

"You have found nothing concrete, nothing to locate these mercenaries so far, Henri?'' Chantal wanted to know.

"Nothing. A possible lead to Zaïre, so we contacted Sorel. No one knows more about Zaïre and most of Central Africa than he does. We have worked with him many times since the war. But this time he knows nothing beyond the vague rumors. He is out now following some leads for me. I expect him back tomorrow or the day after. Then we can plan our next move.''

Chantal nodded. "Very well. I suggest we all get some sleep.''

"And I suggest you keep out of sight,'' Baudou said. "We can't be sure of all the employees in this hotel, maybe not even of all Degrange's old comrades. They know about me, but I think it best we keep them thinking you are some kind of prisoner.''

Chantal nodded, and they all went back up into the night one at a time. Carter walked in the darkness with Chantal.

"So you're military intelligence. You didn't tell me.''

"Even the great Nick Carter can't really know every-thing," she grinned.

"Your father?"

Chantal shrugged. "Le Basque cannot know everything either."

"But now he knows," Carter said.

"Yes," the dark-haired woman said, "now he knows." And she vanished into the hotel by a rear door.

Carter waited out in the night for a time and had a cigarette. Then he strolled around to the front, smiled at the old maquis drinking and refighting World War II in the bar, and went up to his room. He was bone tired, and undressed quickly and slid into bed.

And froze.

Something was in his room.

Movement across the floor, soft and light, like an animal crawling toward his bed, a snake slithering softly yet heavily across the room.

ELEVEN

Carter lay rigid.

Listened.

It moved slowly, soundlessly.

Almost without sound. But not quite.

A soft sibilance across the polished wood floor of the large room, dragging.

The faint brush of slow movement over the delicate Dhurrie rug between the mosquito-net-canopied bed and the open window with its curtains blowing lightly in the hot night.

An all but unheard *click, click, click,* as of small claws scraping against the wood of the smooth floor.

Closer.

Sweat poured off Carter's face in the hot night, down his chest brushed by the light jungle wind.

His right hand moved toward the edge of the pillow beneath his sweat-soaked head.

The hand moved as if unattached to his body, on its own. Imperceptible. His body lying motionless, breathing lightly, unaware of anything but sleep.

His hand came to the edge of the pillow where Wilhelmina and Hugo waited.

The soundless sense of movement in the silver light of the large room was almost at the bed. Almost beneath his limp and sleeping left hand. Directly below the bed where his immobile body sweated.

There was a small metallic scrape, like claws on the metal of the bed.

His hand closed over Hugo, held the stiletto.

The bed shook then sagged as a weight touched it.

Carter tensed every muscle . . . and whipped Hugo across his body at the pale thing down on the floor!

Wilhelmina was in his hand, the Luger aimed at the pale, naked, sprawled figure and wide eyes of Chantal.

Dark, startled, violent eyes that stared at him in the dim bedroom lit only by the distant moon beyond the open windows.

Chantal. Naked.

The stiletto stood buried three inches in the polished wood floor three feet to her right.

Where she had been until, in a split second, she had rolled away to lie sprawled on her back, breasts quivering.

Carter was on his knees now on the bed, naked, Wilhelmina in both hands aimed at her eyes.

She looked at the Luger.

"A bad idea?"

Carter wiped the sweat from his face, and lowered the Luger.

"Very bad."

She smiled and shrugged. "A small surprise."

Carter breathed slowly. "I'm surprised."

He replaced the gun beneath his pillow, then stared at her in the silvery glow of moonlight from the open windows where the curtains blew softly. Chantal still lay sprawled on her back, her dark hair like a great halo around her intense face, her legs wide open to the wedge of black in the moon shadows, her breasts flowing full on her rib cage and the small bandage over the wound from Tangier.

Carter left Hugo embedded in the floor and went down to the naked woman.

She opened wider for him, spread like a great hunger on the polished wood of the floor in the moonlight.

In her.

Deeper into her than Hugo into the floor. Deeper than a knife and hotter than the African night. Savage in her. Savage cries as she shuddered again and again, cries as low and wild as the hunting growl of a leopard out in the towering jungle. Sweat slick on the polished floor, sliding and straining until the wall stopped them and she thrust back as hard as his straining into her. Again and again and again and . . .

The jungle breeze blew cool on their sweat where they lay in silence on the polished floor against the wall under the open windows. They lay and listened to the night sounds: the cries of the night birds, the cough of the hunting leopard, the chattering of monkeys, the scream of some small animal in the jaws of a predator.

Carter picked her up, her breasts heavy against his chest, her face buried in his shoulder, the dark hair flowing down over her body, and carried her to the bed. She wrapped her legs around his hips, and they fell on the bed locked like a single animal in the luminous night. On top, she moaned and writhed against him, thrusting her locked hips, crying out as the spasms surged through her. Her hair swirled around her head until at last he exploded through her and the whole night seemed to shudder and tremble and there was no sound anywhere but the pounding of the blood in his ears.

Carter opened his eyes. This time the sound was not in the room. It was outside. Somewhere below the open windows.

"What is it, Nick?"

Chantal lay with her eyes open beside him, alert and listening.

"Someone is under the window," Carter said. Wilhelmina was in his hand.

They listened. The sound came again. A rustling and a click of metal against wood, and then the rustling slowly faded away. They got out of bed and stepped lightly across the room, dark now with the moon gone, to the open windows.

"Did you notice that Degrange left a guard on the front gate after we came in?" Carter asked.

"I noticed. There *is* a lot of unrest in Zaïre—envy of rich foreigners."

Carter ducked. "Down!"

They crouched beneath the windows, then slowly raised up.

"There," Carter whispered.

Below the windows two armed hotel attendants came into view, stopped to speak to each other, and moved off out of sight.

"And there," Carter said.

Guards sat on platforms behind the far-off wall that surrounded the grounds, stood under all the windows, were spread out among the trees and thick growth of the junglelike grounds beyond the lawn.

"They have a pretty tight net all around the hotel," Chantal said.

"Yeah," Carter said. "The bellboys and room service attendants seem to know a lot about handling weapons."

"What does it mean, Nick?"

"I'm not sure, but that little trick of getting us arrested and then coming to bust us out means that as far as anyone knows, we went to a Zaïrean military jail and are still there. We went in and vanished, no one knows where."

"For their protection."

"Against whom?" Carter said.

"A normal precaution."

"Maybe," Carter said. "But the way it works out, not only does no one know they're with us, no one knows we're with them."

"The guards could, because Sorel is working with our intelligence. That room Henri Baudou took us to is a communications center for military intelligence. The Zaïre government wouldn't like it if they found it. Perhaps the guards are ours."

"French military intelligence?"

"It would not surprise me."

"Wouldn't Baudou have told you?"

"Not necessarily, Nick. We have our own operations."

"Let's find out," Carter said, looking at her where she stood slim and naked. "You can wear my clothes."

She smiled. "That would be romantic, Killmaster, but mine are on your balcony."

Silently, the dark-haired agent slipped out to the balcony, returned, and dressed in a tight-fitting black jump suit, slid a small Ingram submachine gun not much larger than a pistol from a secret pocket on the leg, checked it, returned it, and nodded to Carter. All in black himself, the Killmaster observed the movements of the guards below.

"We need to draw away the three below the windows on this side," he said.

"I'll go down and start a disturbance in the front."

"Too risky," Carter decided. "You could be spotted or caught and we wouldn't find out what we need: who and what and why."

"Then what can we do?"

"Go down from the balcony when the guards aren't looking. There's plenty of cover close to the hotel."

"And how do we make sure the guards aren't looking?"

"That's my job. You get ready to move fast to the balcony and down."

Carter crossed the room to his suitcase, opened it, and pressed a strip of metal. From a secret compartment inside the steel frame he took a long, slender rod. Chantal watched him closely as he went to the windows, made sure the sentries below were looking the other way, then aimed the slender rod toward the nearest trees and jungle growth.

"Ready?"

At the other side of the windows out onto the balcony, she nodded, watching him.

There was a faint *pop*, and Carter held less than half of the slender metal rod. Moments later there was a bright point of light and the sound of something thrashing in the thick jungle growth beyond the hotel.

Below, the three sentries ran toward the noise, waving to each other to spread out as they approached the thick undergrowth. Carter and Chantal jumped out onto the second-floor balcony, lowered themselves over the edge, and dropped to the ground behind the high bushes that grew close against the old hotel.

The sentries returned and stood together under Carter's window where the two agents crouched hidden behind the heavy bushes in the now moonless night.

"What was it?" one of them said. A short, stocky man in his forties with a missing finger on his left hand, he wore the uniform of a hotel bellboy.

"Nick!" Chantal breathed.

Carter nodded. The man had spoken in German.

"How the hell should I know?" the second said. "But it was sure something. We'd better report it."

He was a skinny younger man, not much more than thirty, also dressed in the blue and white uniform of the hotel. He spoke in English.

"He'll have our asses if we leave our posts," the third said. Much older, thick through the middle, he was dressed as a gardener and had also spoken in English but with a strong accent.

In the bushes Carter whispered, "Hungarian?"

"I think so," Chantal agreed.

The three guards stood indecisive, looking around them in the night, then started back toward where the noise and light had come from but where they had found nothing.

"All right. One of us goes, the other two cover his post," the German said.

"I'll go," the skinny younger one said. "I ain't scared."

"We are not scared either, Canadian," the older man said. "We are just more experienced than you. One does not leave one's post unguarded."

"So guard it, old man," the skinny Canadian said, and disappeared into the night.

The other two took up positions where they covered

all three areas beneath the hotel windows, leaving a seam between them and the sentries around the corners of the vast white hotel with its red tile roof. Carter and Chantal slipped silently along the wall of the hotel behind the shrubbery.

"Recognize any of them?" Carter asked.

"No. They're not military intelligence."

When the German and the sentry around the corner guarding the side of the hotel were both looking away, Carter and Chantal broke across the narrow open space between the hotel and the first line of trees that bordered the side lawn. From there they worked their way around the entire hotel, observing the sentries under all the windows and at the front and side doors. They were all dressed as bellboys, room service attendants, gardeners, maintenance men, waiters and kitchen workers. All ages and sizes.

"Remember those blacks at the attack outside Tangier? The Americans and Cubans?" Chantal said.

Carter nodded.

They continued to work their way around, observing the sentries on the wall and at the front gate. They were the same: men of all ages, races, nationalities. All were dressed as members of the hotel staff.

"What does it mean, Nick?" Chantal wondered. "Is it just because Sorel is working with military intelligence?"

"Maybe. Or maybe he doesn't even know what goes on when he's not here."

"Degrange?"

"Possible. What about that Captain Baudou?"

"Henri has an impeccable record."

"People can change."

"I know, but what possible reason could Henri have for recruiting a private army?"

"The same as anyone—greed, money, power, a change of political heart. How well do you really know him, Chantal?"

"As well as any of us know each other in intelligence work, Nick. You know we don't—"

"Quiet!"

Carter gripped her arm hard. He listened in the dark night. Somewhere in the hotel basement a faint bell or low buzzer rang, sounding like an electronic alarm. Feet were running straight toward where they lay hidden among the bushes and trees between the wall and the lawn. Henri Baudou's voice called through the night.

"Spread out! Surround the area."

Where the two agents lay hidden in the thick jungle growth, Chantal's eyes searched the darkness.

"They're all around us!"

Carter swore. "We must have tripped some kind of alarm."

"What can we do?" Chantal said calmly, listening to the running feet coming closer.

"Nothing," Carter said grimly. "They've got us surrounded."

"Yes," Chantal said, and suddenly stood up.

She stood up in the night and called out into the darkness, "Here, Henri! Over here is what you want."

TWELVE

"Don't move," she whispered to Carter.

Carter lay motionless as he watched her stand over him smiling off into the night toward where Henri Baudou and the armed sentries approached warily.

She smiled toward Baudou, whispering down to Carter: "We can't shoot our way out. As far as I know they're on our side. I'll have to talk our way out."

And she walked out of the thick jungle growth shouting, "It is only me, Henri! You caught me."

On the dark lawn Henri Baudou stopped, the M-16 in his hand still aimed toward the brush and Chantal. The military intelligence captain eyed her suspiciously. His quick eyes searched on both sides and behind her for some trick, for someone else, for danger. The heavily armed guards in their various hotel costumes circled toward her on both sides. Baudou advanced slowly.

"What do you think you're up to, Chantal?"

"My job, Henri," the dark-haired woman said.

"Job? What job is that?"

"The job of knowing what is going on."

"Here?" Baudou said. "I told you what was going on here."

Chantal walked out of the dense growth toward Baudou, her gaze steady on his face. Intense. Sincere. In the dense underbrush among the trees Carter barely breathed. He held Wilhelmina, waited, and watched. The ranks of the sentries came between Chantal and where Carter lay. They turned and followed her toward Baudou, their backs to him. Carter let out a slow breath.

"Did you, Henri?" her voice said, out in the open on the lawn now. Carter could barely glimpse her through the armed men who had encircled her and closed in. "When we came in with Degrange and the old resistance fighters who rescued us, Degrange put a guard at the gate. Later, when you had us taken down to your communications room, I noticed how at ease the hotel employees seemed to be with guns." She moved closer to Baudou the entire time she was talking, moving away from the thick growth under the trees, pulling the armed men along behind her. "When I went to bed I couldn't sleep right away, so I got up to sit on the balcony and have a cigarette. That was when I noticed the guard under my windows."

Henri Baudou watched her. "Did you?"

"I did, and I wondered about that," Chantal said, continuing to walk past Baudou who fell into step beside her. "Then I saw the sentries under all the windows. Sentries all over the hotel grounds. And that was when I decided to find out who they were and why they were there."

"You could have simply come and asked me," Baudou said.

"Could I?"

Baudou shrugged in the dark, moonless, early morning hours. "Perhaps not. So, what have you learned?"

"That they come from many countries, the armed men here. They are of many ages, even many races. They are not our people, Henri, and they are not amateurs. That is what I thought I saw when Degrange brought us here, and that was why I had to check up, and that is what I've been doing."

"Alone?"

"You think I'm afraid of the dark? I need a man with me perhaps?"

"No, I doubt that you need anyone with you," Baudou said. "That kind of thing can be dangerous, though. You could have trusted me—decided I knew what I was doing."

Chantal shook her head. "No, you would have done the same thing, Henri. It is our job to know; it was my job to find out. If I hadn't, you would probably have reported me."

Baudou laughed. "Yes, I would have. You always were a good agent, Chantal."

"So were you, Henri. What is going on here? Is it Degrange? I have been suspicious of him from the beginning. He acts as if he is in command here, owns the hotel. Where is Sorel? Is he fooling Sorel? Some scheme of his own? Perhaps he knows more about the American aid and the mercenaries than he has told anyone. Maybe he is fooling Sorel and you too, Henri."

"Let's go to my room. I'll explain it all to you." Baudou turned and barked orders to the sentries.

They dispersed into the blackness of the heavy African night, moving with the skill and speed of trained men. Baudou led Chantal back across the lawn to the hotel.

• • •

From where he lay in the thick undergrowth, Carter watched the sentries scatter and return to their posts at the walls, under the windows, and at the doors of the vast, silent hotel. He watched Chantal go toward the hotel with Captain Baudou.

The night became motionless. He heard only the sounds of the jungle slowly returning beyond the walls: the chattering of the monkeys, the cries of nocturnal birds, the soft rustling of the stealthy predators.

Carter got up and moved through the dense growth as quietly as any jungle cat.

He circled in the shadows under the trees between the lawn and the wall until he reached a spot at the rear of the hotel where the open space was small. On his belly he crawled across the narrow rear lawn in the moonless dark. The single sentry at the rear door heard nothing; he stood smoking, a red point of waxing and waning light.

Carter found an open window at the side of the sleeping hotel, climbed in, and slipped through the room soundlessly as two figures in the mosquito-net-enclosed bed snored and tossed in their sleep.

Out in the dim corridor, he trotted lightly past the closed doors until he reached the echoing lobby.

The registration desk was deserted.

Carter crossed the empty lobby without a sound and found the registration cards. Henri Baudou was in Room 29. That would be the second floor front.

Back out in the cover of the dark night, he swiftly climbed up the vines and drainpipes and balconies to the red-tiled roof. He ran along the roof like a shadow until he located his own room, then he retraced his steps to Baudou's windows. There was light through the French captain's window out onto his balcony.

Carter dropped lightly from the roof to the third-floor balcony and to Baudou's balcony. He crouched in the shadows outside the French captain's windows.

". . . you would have found out the rest if you hadn't tripped that alarm."

Henri Baudou's voice could be heard clearly from the balcony in the quiet and windless early-morning hour. Inside the room the Frenchman was seated on a rattan couch, a glass of cognac in his hand, his shirt unbuttoned. Chantal sat in a straight chair, her slim body outlined in the black jump suit, the deadly Ingram invisible in its hidden pocket on her leg.

"Tell me the rest," she said.

Baudou leaned forward, intense, the cognac glass held between his legs. "You were right about the sentries, the hotel staff. They are all professional, all soldiers. From every country on earth, just about."

Chantal watched him. "Why, Henri?"

"It was Sorel's idea," Baudou said, his voice admiring, almost in awe. "There has always been a lot of unrest down here, ever since independence and the death of Lumumba and the troubles in Katanga over the years, and the hotel was often on the edge of real trouble. So Sorel wanted guards, and he got the idea of rounding up bored former soldiers—from anywhere—and hiring them to work here at the hotel and act as guards too! He got his guards and they got the jobs they needed. With the unsettled state of Zaïre, and the antagonism to Europeans, they've come in handy many times to save the hotel and the guests."

"That's all?" Chantal said.

Baudou shook his head. "No, it was just the beginning. Once Sorel had all the old guerrillas down here, he started to use them and the hotel to rescue and shelter hundreds of Europeans and natives from the constant African civil wars, insurrections, revolutions and counterrevolutions.''

''That sounds more like the man my father served under. He saved so many people from the Nazis during the war.''

Baudou nodded. ''Quite a man, Sorel. He knows you must have organization and strength to help people, just as they had in the French underground. Unorganized, weak, you can do nothing. Strength is needed to accomplish anything worthwhile, and that's what I'm doing here.''

Carter watched the Frenchman take a long gulp of his cognac. He saw Chantal move in her chair, never taking her dark eyes from Baudou's face.

''What are you doing here, Henri?''

''When we traced the last rumor about the force of mercenaries to Zaïre, and heard about shipments of some sophisticated weapons from the USSR going through Tangier to Zaïre, I was sent down to enlist Sorel's help once more. He knows everything there is to know about Africa, Chantal. We needed his help.''

''What have you learned?''

Baudou shook his head. ''Nothing. Sorel has been everywhere, sent his people—but so far, nothing. I'm beginning to think Degrange is right: the mercenaries are mythical—invented to cover the actions of the governments that steal the aid material and dollars from their own starving people to fatten their 'retirement' accounts in Swiss banks.''

''Then what about the shipments from Russia?'' Chantal said.

''They could contain anything. Gold, for example.

The Soviets have plenty of gold to pay for what they want."

Chantal shook her head. "They could sell that American material on any black market for more than they would get selling it to one buyer, Henri."

"True, but they wouldn't get gold, and it would be a lot of trouble and much more risky. Besides, I suspect a lot of America aid cash is missing too, and that would be in dollars. To spend it, whoever has it would have to launder it, and what better way than getting gold for it from the Soviets? A single package deal. They take a loss on the material to get the laundering of the cash. Everyone wins."

"Then who are the people who attacked Nick twice?"

"Are you sure anyone did?"

"I was there the second time in Tangier."

"It could have been arranged."

"He killed fifteen of them with our gunship, Henri."

"I have heard of worse being done to convince someone of a ruse," Baudou said. "Just who is this Nicholas Meyer? Degrange thinks he's more than CIA —something else . . ."

Chantal stood up. "Degrange may be something else himself. I don't trust that man, Henri. I don't think my father does either. Are you sure of him?"

"He's been with Sorel since the war."

She nodded. "It must be my imagination then. We'd better get some sleep. With luck, Sorel will return and we can decide what to do next."

"Chantal?" Baudou said.

Carter watched her stop at the door of the room.

"You could sleep here."

She smiled. "Why, thank you, Henri, but it's been a long night. Perhaps some other time."

On the balcony Carter grinned, waited until Henri Baudou walked to the door to see Chantal out, then quickly climbed back up to the roof like some dark cat.

On the red tile he watched the sentries change as a thin gold line of dawn spread across the great flat African land over the sand hills to the north. He moved along the roof to his own room. Below, the two sentries, one coming on and the other going off, stood in conversation. One of them faced the hotel in the slowly lightening dawn, and every now and then he looked up as if at the balcony of Carter's room.

The Killmaster swore to himself. Every minute increased the danger of discovery as the dawn light grew. Moving quickly, Carter slipped across the roof to the dark side of the building and dropped down to the balcony of a silent room. He saw no guards, swung over, and dropped to the next balcony and onto the ground. In the shadows of the shrubs against the hotel, he hurried along looking for an open window and an empty room.

And stopped.

Through a closed window of what looked like an office on the ground floor, a man sat at a desk working on the keyboard of a computer, studying the lines that appeared on the lighted screen.

A smallish man, slim and narrow and very erect in his chair. Imperious. A cold, hard face like some mountain eagle, lined and craggy, with white hair and a thick salt-and-pepper mustache. A gaunt face, commanding.

The face Carter had last seen standing on a high rock in Ethiopia looking down on where Carter lay hidden from the hillside of gunfire aimed at him by the unknown soldiers in gray!

The Killmaster found an open window and an empty

room, climbed in, and ran softly through to the rear corridor of the hotel behind the registration desk. He drew his Luger and moved, swift and silent, along the corridor to the door of the room where the man with the gaunt eagle's face worked on the computer. It was marked Accounting.

Carter tried the knob.

There was a soft click. The door was unlocked.

Carter flung the door open and jumped in, both hands on Wilhelmina out in front of him.

The room was empty, the computer dark.

He put his hand on the computer. It was still warm.

But the room was empty.

He stood there for some time, thinking, and then closed the door behind him and slipped along to the rear stairs and up to his room.

The dawn was full now as he undressed and lay down in bed once more. And thought about the white-haired, ramrod-straight, commanding man he had now seen twice.

THIRTEEN

Nick Carter slept for three hours, Wilhelmina in his hand under the thin sheet in the growing heat of the African morning. Awake, he concentrated his power in meditation, unaware of time or space for fifteen minutes.

Released, refreshed, he listened to the sounds of the hotel, the rhythm and pulse around him. All was quiet and normal, the lazy voices and movements of a resort hotel at breakfast on the lawn, in the arbors, the light footsteps in the corridors going nowhere in particular.

He got up and looked out. The sentries were gone from under the windows, but he saw them still on the walls and at the gates in the distance across the lawn and through the trees and thick jungle growth.

In the shower he thought about Henri Baudou's story. It could be true; Baudou had sounded sincere. Or Baudou could be a hell of a good actor and part of what was going on. Baudou or Degrange or both, and who was the white-haired man last night?

Maybe Hawk could come up with some identification, something on Degrange or Baudou, but there was no telephone in the room, and to reach Hawk now he needed a telephone or radio transmitter.

In fresh clothes, his weapons in their places, Carter left the room. The hotel corridors were bright and peaceful, the few tourists smiling at him eagerly and a little nervously as they passed, the way tourists always do in strange countries. Down the broad stairs to the lobby he saw Le Basque and the other old maquis in the dining room arguing heatedly about something.

There were no house telephones or booths.

At the registration desk the uniformed desk clerk smiled. "Yes, sir?"

"Where can I make a telephone call?"

"In the office there, sir. Just dial three for an outside line."

Carter thanked the smiling man. He recognized him as one of the guards who had answered the alarm last night. In the office he left the door open. It was always better to lower his voice and leave the door open so no one could come close enough to eavesdrop. He used his small anti-bug detection device. The phone wasn't bugged.

He dialed three, waited for the change in tone, then punched in the secret numbers for the worldwide AXE computer.

The phone rang . . . and the dial tone returned.

Carter muttered over the technical incompetence of most Third World countries, punched three again, and dialed in his secret code numbers.

Ring . . . dial tone.

The Killmaster stared at the black instrument. Then he looked out the open door to where the desk clerk seemed to be watching him. The clerk busied himself quickly with some paper shuffling.

Carter dialed once more.

Ring . . . dial tone.

He hung up and walked out to the desk.

"Okay, what do I have to do to make a phone call?"

The clerk looked up, surprised. "As I said, sir, just dial three—"

"I get one ring, then the dial tone. What's going on?"

"One . . . ? Oh, were you trying to dial out of the country, sir?"

"That's not—"

"Because if you were, sir, that is blocked. No calls can be made out of the country from here. You have to go to the central exchange in Kinshasa."

"Whose idea is that?"

"I wouldn't know, sir. I just work here."

Frustrated, Carter went into the dining room. Le Basque waved him over. Chantal was wearing a trim safari outfit, including bush hat and a large leather handbag big enough to hold an Ingram.

"Baudou?" Carter said as she sat down.

"Gone into Kinshasa," Le Basque said. "I hear you two had an adventure last night."

"Yes," Carter said, looking at Chantal. "You believe Baudou?"

The waiter was there before she could answer. Carter ordered a mushroom omelette, fruit, toast, and coffee. The waiter hovered, writing endlessly.

"Now?" Carter said.

The waiter glared and left.

"He was one of the sentries last night," Chantal said. "I have no reason to not believe Henri."

"Degrange? Where is he?" Carter asked.

"Kinshasa," Le Basque said.

"With Baudou?"

"No. Degrange went in last night soon after dinner."

"To do what?"

"He didn't confide in me," Le Basque said.

The waiter returned with Carter's breakfast and removed Le Basque's and Chantal's dishes. Carter watched the waiter. The waiter left.

"I saw a man in the Accounting office back behind the registration desk last night," Carter said. "A small man, thin. Looked hard as a rock despite his white hair. Face like an eagle, lined and craggy, gaunt. A thick gray mustache, almost white. Cool and hard, I'd say. Commanding. Either of you know him?"

Chantal shook her head. "I don't recognize him, Nick. He sounds like someone I'd like to know, but I don't."

"You haven't seen him around the hotel? Perhaps in Paris?"

"No."

"Some connection to Lyons before he died?"

"No. I just don't know anyone like that."

Le Basque had said nothing. Carter looked at him. The old fighter and smuggler was pale under his mustache.

"Le Basque?" Carter said.

"You saw this man last night? In the hotel?"

"Working on a computer. He must have seen me, because when I tried to reach him in the office he was gone. The computer was still warm."

"Describe him again. Everything."

Carter did.

"Last night . . ." Le Basque said.

Chantal said, "What's wrong, Papa? What is it?"

"I'm not sure," Le Basque said. "Nick, did this man have a scar on the left ear? Another, perhaps, over the right eye?"

"I didn't see any scars, but I wasn't that close either time."

"Either time?" Le Basque repeated.

Carter told them about the commander on the rock in Ethiopia. "What's bothering you, *mon ami?*"

Le Basque's voice was low, uneasy. "That description fits Julian Sorel himself. If he has those scars—"

The old maquis didn't go on.

"Sorel?" Carter said. "Why would he be hiding from us? What was he doing with soldiers in Ethiopia?"

"We don't know he's doing either, not for certain," Le Basque said.

"Whoever Nick saw *is* hiding," Chantal said. "No one else has seen him."

"Tell me about Sorel," Carter said.

Le Basque looked out the windows at the broad front lawn and the African jungle beyond the wall and a lot farther than that, perhaps all the way to France forty or more years ago. "He would not be hiding, no. He never hid. He evaded, fooled the enemy, but they always knew he was there."

Le Basque watched one of the bellboys crossing the lawn in the hot sun. "The first time I met him I was an angry boy running from the Gestapo and our own Vichy police. They had shot my father, and I had killed two SS men in return and run into the night with the dogs after me. Sorel saved me. Without him I would have been caught within hours. He saved me and taught me the need of organization, of cooperation, of working in a selfless group. He taught me that a man alone is always the victim, that to defeat Nazis or anyone you must organize, join together. He took me in, protected me, taught me how to fight the power of a faceless enemy, defeat mindless efficiency such as the Nazis. How to find their weak points and use those weaknesses to destroy them."

The waiter had moved closer, busy and hovering. Le Basque turned to smile at him. "Perhaps some more coffee, eh, young man?"

The waiter scowled but left. Le Basque returned his gaze to the lawn through the windows, to those long-ago days. "He was a great leader, guerrilla tactician, even strategist. Another time, another place, he would have been a general. We killed many SS men, even Gestapo. We destroyed, we disrupted, we undermined them. Twice we even attacked the mighty 'Das Reich' Waffen SS division. Many of us died, many were captured, tortured. Sorel himself was captured four, five times. Once even by Klaus Barbie, our beautiful Butcher of Lyons, eh? But always he escaped, defied them."

The waiter brought the coffee. Le Basque nodded and waved him away. "Sorel always escaped and he helped so many others to escape. Others he helped out of the country, out of danger, but he himself stayed. So many other resistance units were discovered, attacked, destroyed, scattered, all running with the SS hanging black over them. Sorel got them out to Switzerland, to the sea and the English, to Spain and the secret antifascist underground. So many comrades he saved, and led us so well in our fights that we were never discovered, never defeated."

There was pride in the old man's voice, a shine to his eyes as he remembered those days and his commandant.

"What happened at the end?" Carter asked.

"Ah, that was his most dazzling triumph. We were fighting near Lyons, ambushing the Nazis as they fled, and Sorel was captured once more and by Klaus Barbie again. We were sure it was the end for the commandant—he would be murdered, or at best taken to Germany and killed there—but once more he escaped." The old man's eyes gleamed as he gulped his coffee. "He rejoined us, and there were many fighters lost those last days, but the commandant kept us safe and then marched right out in the open to meet the Americans. He said we had to meet the Americans as fighters, as victors, not as beaten victims who had to be saved. We had saved ourselves, and he marched us through his own home village to the Americans. The Germans did not touch us!''

The moment of triumph was all over the old man's face. Chantal smiled as if she wished she had been there. Carter watched Le Basque.

"Then?" the Killmaster prompted. "When the war was over?"

Le Basque sighed and shook his head, still partly lost in the dream of his memory. Whether it had really been like that or not, Carter could only guess.

"It was hard on the men, my mother told me," Chantal added. "Many could not adjust. They had been boys in 1940, and six years later they were men who had missed their opportunities. They had no skills, no training, no careers except to destroy and kill."

Le Basque nodded. "Sorel had lost his family, his friends in the resistance, everything. He could not stand the France that came with victory, he told me. The petty bickering, the politicians who crawled out of hiding, the fat men who had grown rich while he fought. So he came here to the Congo—where they spoke French but were not French—and worked and soon opened this hotel, and he has been here ever since."

"Still saving people, if Baudou is right," Chantal said. "Still rescuing people. And working all along for our military intelligence whenever we needed some secret help in Africa."

"Working with you too, Le Basque?" Carter asked.

"No. We have not worked with the commandant

since the war. We have met in Paris, but he went his own way down here with his own people.''

"Degrange? Was he in your unit in the war?''

Le Basque nodded. "The commandant's most trusted lieutenant.''

"Why not all of you, then?''

Le Basque shrugged. "We went in different directions, Killmaster.''

"Why would Sorel hide from you now? From us?''

"There will be a good answer. *If* he is hiding. *If* it is the commandant you saw. I know there will be a simple answer.''

Carter watched the old maquis. "I hope so.''

"Nick!'' Chantal whispered.

Carter turned to see where she was looking. Henri Baudou had come in the front door. The French military intelligence captain stood and looked around urgently. When he saw Le Basque and Chantal, he hurried across the dining room.

"Degrange just received a message from commandant Sorel in Lubumbashi. The commandant thinks he has located some of the Soviet boxes from Tangier down in Katanga. We will all go!''

"Where is Degrange?'' Carter asked.

"He just got back from Kinshasa. He's been trying to get Le Basque's gunship out of Zaïrean hands since last night, but they won't let it go. We'll have to take a charter flight down to Lubumbashi.''

"Who is all of us, Baudou?'' Le Basque wanted to know.

"Your people, myself, and Degrange and a few of his old maquis. That's all.''

"Let's go,'' Le Basque said.

FOURTEEN

The private landing field was a mile north of the hotel; Carter had no chance to reach a telephone or radio. A chartered plane, a small executive jet, was there waiting for them. Degrange sat with Henri Baudou at the front, his old Zaïre-based maquis scattered among the seats of the small aircraft. Le Basque and his six companions sat together in seats in the center of the jet.

Carter observed the arrangement.

"What's bothering you?" Chantal whispered beside him.

"I'm not sure. Have you noticed how Degrange's men are scattered around the plane?"

Chantal looked around. "There aren't that many seats, Nick. We got these seven together—they had to take what were left."

"Maybe," Carter said. "So you think we were just lucky to get these seven together?"

"I think I'd be more suspicious if they'd separated us."

"That could be," Carter admitted. He glanced around. Degrange and Baudou seemed deep in discus-

117

sion. Do you have a radio transmitter?"

"The Zaïreans took it," Chantal said.

"Degrange didn't rescue it?"

"No."

"How about your father and his men?"

"Only on the C-47."

Carter considered the closed door of the pilot's cabin, in front of which Degrange and Captain Baudou were talking. There would be a radio in the cockpit, but on the small jet it would be impossible to talk to Hawk without anyone else hearing him. He decided against it. With any luck he could contact Hawk after meeting with Sorel.

"You are wondering if Sorel is being honest with us, Killmaster?"

Le Basque leaned over and spoke close and low into Carter's ear.

"I don't know what Sorel is doing," Carter said, "but I intend to find out."

"I think," Le Basque said, "that when we land in Lubumbashi, I shall insist that we meet the commandant first in some public place, eh? Before we talk to him about your business."

"I'm not sure we're in any position to insist on much," Carter said, nodding to the Zaïrean maquis all around them in the jet.

"We have our weapons, Killmaster," Le Basque said. "The moment this aircraft comes down in Lubumbashi we will assume control. Are you with us?"

Carter nodded. "I'll handle Degrange, and Chantal can take Captain Baudou until we're sure where he stands."

"Yes, agreed," Le Basque said, nodding. "Then we understand? I will give the signal."

The old man sat back in his seat, closed his eyes, and

slept or pretended to sleep. Carter looked out the window at the endless sea of jungle below. He watched the wide green flow beneath the wings, and the rivers that were barely visible as the lush forest closed over them. At the same time, he watched Baudou and Degrange up at the front of the small jet. They were still deep in conversation, apparently unaware of what was happening inside the plane.

The jet flew on, eating up the miles like a bullet in contrast to the lumbering old C-47, but with less cargo space and a lot less flexibility. Lubumbashi—the former Elisabethville—capital of the copper-rich Katanga province Moishe Tshombe had tried to separate from Zaïre for the benefit of the European metal companies, was at the extreme opposite end of the country, historically in another world yet less than a thousand miles and a few hours away from Kinshasa as the jet flew.

Soon the jungle began to thin out into the high savanna and scrub woodland of the south and east of Zaïre, the great central plateau of southern Africa. Trees dotted the plains of coarse grass and thick underbrush, and here and there was some scattered real grassland. There was a lake and a large river, and then the beginnings of a more populated, more civilized-looking area.

Carter looked at his watch. They would be landing in Lubumbashi in less then fifteen minutes if his calculations were correct. He stretched and yawned and glanced around the interior of the jet. Degrange and Henri Baudou were still talking, oblivious to anything around them, and the old maquis were dozing in their seats. He leaned back, checked his weapons casually, and looked out. . . .

The ground was no more than a few hundred feet below, and the jet was slowing rapidly!

Even as Carter looked out, the plane seemed to stop in midair as the flaps went down.

They were landing!

Carter strained to look in all directions, but he saw no sign of a major city or even a village.

Only a long concrete runway of what looked like an abandoned military airstrip loomed ahead.

Le Basque looked out beside him. "What do you think it is?"

"It's not Lubumbashi," Carter said.

The jet touched down, bounced, touched again, and raced along the empty runway toward a large woods of tall trees.

"I think it is time," Le Basque said.

"Look!" Chantal said.

All along the runway, and out of the woods, ranks of gray-uniformed soldiers armed with automatic weapons appeared, running to surround the jet as it came to a slow stop. Before and behind. Everywhere. Hundreds of the gray bush uniforms.

"Now!" Le Basque said.

Carter and Chantal moved toward the front to cover Degrange and Baudou.

The other Parisian maquis jumped up.

The door to the pilot's cabin opened. Three men with submachine guns jumped through. A fourth man came behind them.

The small, slim, craggy, white-haired man with the cold eyes and commanding face. In the same gray field uniform and paratrooper boots, a blue beret on his white hair. With the thick gray mustache, and the gaunt face of a mountain eagle.

"I would not suggest an attempt," the gaunt man said in a low, thin voice.

The Zaïrean maquis were on their feet, their weapons

ready. Degrange had a gun. Only Henri Baudou seemed surprised, confused.

"What the hell—?"

"Sit down, fool," the gaunt man said.

Baudou blinked and grabbed his pistol from his pocket. "Chantal, take—"

The craggy, white-haired man raised his Uzi and fired a single burst that flung Baudou back against the window, spraying blood across the chairs and Degrange. The French captain was dead before his body hit the floor.

"His usefulness was over," Degrange said, wiping the dead man's blood from his face.

Outside the soldiers ringed the jet like a vise. Carter dropped Wilhelmina. Chantal handed her Ingram to Degrange. The Parisian maquis raised their hands. Le Basque stepped to the white-haired man with the hawk face and held out his pistol.

"You want my gun, Commandant Sorel? Take it. Kill me. I did not think I would see this day."

The gaunt man, Julien Sorel, shrugged. "Times change, Etienne."

Naked, Nick Carter sat in the dark cell. He tried to remember how he had gotten there.

He remembered the gray soldiers outside the jet. The old maquis commandant, Julien Sorel. Out of the pilot's cabin. Guns. Blood. The French captain.

Then . . . ?

Trucks. Covered and closed. Trucks and . . . a long ride, a long, long time . . . night . . . odor . . . an odor! A smoke! Gas! Gas in the closed truck! Yes . . . gas, that was . . . .

In the darkness Carter shook his head and took a deep breath.

That was it. Gassed in the truck.

Now, he was naked in this dark cell.

And he'd been stripped somewhere, sometime.

He breathed deeply. Long, slow breaths. Over and over. His head cleared, and the details of the cell slowly emerged from the darkness. Stone walls. Stone ceiling no more than a foot over his head. He searched slowly, but there were no windows. A metal door. Solid, seamless, without hinges or visible lock or knob.

No furniture.

A mattress on the floor.

No drains.

Nothing.

Carter breathed deep and slow. There was nothing he could see in the stone cell to allow escape, and they had stripped him, leaving him no weapons or tools.

He breathed, and listened to the sounds beyond the steel door. He heard footsteps pacing slowly with the measured and bored tread of a guard. Water dripping. The faint sound of some prisoner singing very softly. Something that tapped, and tapped and . . . tapped?

Carter listened.

The tapping continued. Staccato. Irregular. Long and short. A rhythm, persistent, from the next cell. Over and over.

A code.

Morse code.

Carter listened. It continued . . . *tap-tap-tap . . . tap . . . tap-tap . . . long . . . short . . . Carter . . . Basque . . . Here in the next cell . . . If you hear me, answer. Carter. Basque. Here in the next cell. If you hear me, answer. Carter, Basque. Here in the . . .*

Carter searched the dark as the tapping went on. What was Le Basque tapping with? Or hadn't Sorel stripped his old comrade? Then he saw the bucket.

Everyone had a weakness. Sorel's was a French middle-class upbringing. He could strip the cell, leave nothing but a mattress, have no outlets or drains or no toilet, but he had to leave a bucket for the necessities!

Carter had not had time to need the bucket, so he picked it up and sat it against the wall where the tapping still came. He tapped back:

Carter here. Are you alone?

Yes. Stripped. No weapons.

Same. The others?

All separated. The commandant is efficient. Any way out of your cell?

No. Not a chance. Can only wait for an opportunity if he brings us out of here.

Perhaps you give up too easily, Killmaster. How long have you been awake?

Maybe five minutes, maybe fifteen.

Then you have not eaten. I have. They feed me first, then they feed you. There are two of them, but only one comes into the cell with the food. I will tap when they have fed me. You can be ready.

I'll be ready.

Good.

The tapping ceased, but as Carter sat back against the wall he felt strong, no longer alone in the dark. There were two of them and they had a plan.

He waited in the dark of the cell with the soft padding of the guard outside and the distant dripping of water, the faint singing. Time stands still in the darkness of a cell. There is no time. It stands still and passes in a flash. . . .

Tap . . . tap.

Carter stood, then glided silently across the room to stand behind the door. Footsteps. *Clink, clink.*

The door opened.

The man came in carrying a metal tray and walked toward the mattress.

Carter broke his neck with a single karate chop, caught him and the tray in midair, and lowered them silently to the floor. He went out the door before the second man could raise his rifle, dropped him soundlessly with a kick under the chin, and caught him before he hit the stone corridor.

When he had the keys and the AK-47, he unlocked the next cell and Le Basque came out.

"The other cells," the old man said.

They turned to the next cell.

Doors opened at both ends of the stone corridor.

"You have two seconds to live if you do not place that weapon on the ground, put your hands on the wall, move your feet out, and lean."

It was Julien Sorel's voice.

AK-47s fired at both ends without anyone showing.

Carter laid down the AK-47 and leaned on the corridor wall. Le Basque leaned beside him.

Footsteps came slowly along. Some stood behind them. Some walked on to the cells from which they had escaped.

"Max is okay, but Saul is dead. The tall one broke his neck."

Sorel stood behind them. "Well, I see what I have heard of the Killmaster is correct. Unarmed, naked, he neutralizes two men, one armed. *C'est formidable.*"

"Television cameras," Carter said.

"That's why there were only two guards, only one armed," Le Basque said. "Television surveillance."

"Of course," Sorel said. "One learns new ways over so many years. Stone walls and TV, the old and the new. The power was the Killmaster, but perhaps the plan was my old comrade's, eh? To notice how the feeding was conducted. I should have expected that. Well, no harm done; Saul would have died someday anyway. You may stand away from the wall.''

Carter and Le Basque straightened and turned to face Julien Sorel. The small, slender man now wore an elegant uniform of blue and gold with the insignia of a general. A French uniform.

"Why not a marshal of France, commandant?" Le Basque said.

"Perhaps after my next campaign," Sorel said, and laughed. "Come, Etienne, why not, eh? Did we not fight as well as any general? Plan? Campaign? Who deserved the uniform and the rank more? De Gaulle sitting safe in London? Giraud, posing for pictures in Algiers? Darlan and Pétain licking the boots of the Boche? Perhaps . . . . But never mind. I am sorry about the clothes, but I have heard of the hidden devices of the Killmaster, and I know what you are capable of hiding, eh? So it seemed a fair precaution, and I see how right I was."

"I am not ashamed to be naked, Julien," Le Basque said. "Better that than a stolen uniform."

"As you wish," the slender, white-haired man said with a shrug. "But I have clothes now for you. Put them on, and we will talk."

Sorel turned and walked away in his immaculate uniform. Two gray-uniformed soldiers handed Carter and Le Basque plain gray coveralls and canvas shoes without laces. When they were dressed, the soldiers prodded them up stone steps at the end of the corridor.

FIFTEEN

The silent soldiers pushed them through the door and out into a long, narrow passageway. Carter located the TV camera hidden behind a metal plate with a narrow opening in it, and outside the door was a long passage without doors or windows and another camera at the end. Through the second door was the first guard outside the block of cells. And another long passage without doors or windows.

The passages were carved from solid rock, creating a heavy, silent remoteness as if they were deep in the core of the earth itself. There was a constant hum and the steady movement of a current of air, forced ventilation, the air coming in from somewhere outside, perhaps far above. It reminded Carter of Cheyenne Mountain, the NORAD command deep under the granite outside Colorado Springs.

Ahead now there were shots, whistles, explosions, and the voices of many men shouting in unison. They came out of the last passage into a high-domed cavern where groups of the gray-uniformed soldiers were going through drills, firing on a range, crawling over a combat course with dynamite explosions and barbed wire. Squads were climbing the rock walls, practicing commando tactics, snarling in close-combat exercises.

Ahead, carved out of the sheer rock wall of the great domed cavern, were rows of glassed windows where the higher command officers observed, and banks of electronic equipment flashed and blinked. The soldiers prodded Le Basque and Carter through a door and down more passages in the command sector until they reached a long room with heavy wooden tables and rows of easy chairs. This would be the command room.

"Le Basque!"

Daniel, Karl-Heinz, and the other two old maquis from Paris were already in the room, seated at one of the long tables, dressed in the coveralls and canvas shoes. Julien Sorel sat at the small command table on the raised platform at the far end. Degrange was on one side of him, and a much younger black officer sat on the other. As Carter and Le Basque were pushed to the table with the others, Chantal was dragged into the room by a grinning soldier.

"Take your stupid hands off me, you cockroach!"

The dark-haired woman wore the same coveralls and canvas shoes without laces as the men. Le Basque jumped up, furious.

"Sorel—!"

The white-haired commandant shook his head. "She does a man's work, she is treated as a man. She is no less dangerous than you, Etienne. Regrettable, but there it is."

Le Basque stared at the hawk-faced leader. "You have changed that much, Commandant?"

"No," Sorel said. "I have not changed. The circumstances have changed, so you see now what you had no reason to see then."

Le Basque nodded. "Perhaps there was much I did not see then."

"Perhaps," Sorel agreed. "But we must get down to business. The past is the past. I deal in the present. You have brought this American to me, and he creates a problem that must be dealt with."

"We did not know we were bringing him to you," Le Basque said.

"Of course you did not, yet he is here," Sorel said, "and so are you."

"You knew all along what we were doing," Chantal said, "That was how your soldiers attacked us in Tangier, how Degrange knew we were coming to Zaïre. Someone in our group works for you."

"Of course I knew what you were doing," Sorel agreed, "but no one in Etienne's group works for us. It is only that when anyone from the old resistance wants to know anything that may be happening in Africa, who else would they contact but Commandant Sorel? It was Le Basque's own queries that reached me, told me what you were doing. The airfield was simple enough to determine. Then, Captain Baudou was helpful also, with Miss Borotra's own reports to military intelligence."

Carter nodded. "And you've been watching me since Ethiopia. What was it—did General Tenamu sell American aid material to you?"

Sorel nodded. "The general is a man in need of funds to pay for dreams of power. He will not succeed, but he is useful to us. Unfortunately, your agent, Lyons, traced some of the material in Tangier back to General Tenamu as its source. They had to kill him. I was afraid he had left a message for the 'native' who carried such strange weapons for an Ethiopian refugee. We did not know at first it was the Killmaster himself, Nick Carter."

"You're well informed for a mercenary leader," Carter said.

"Information is as important as weapons today, Killmaster. Surely you know that. An army is lost without full and precise information about anywhere it operates and anyone it operates against."

Le Basque snorted. "A mercenary gang is not an army, Sorel, no matter how clever you think you are."

Sorel's hawk nose pinched, and his dark eyes flashed angrily. "Ten thousand of the best-trained troops on earth are not a gang, Etienne! We are the best, as our resistance unit was the best."

"Best? Thugs for hire? You did not have such a high opinion of mercenaries when we fought together."

"I had many naïve views in those days," Sorel said. "Thugs we are not, for hire we are. For hire to anyone who can pay our fee. Whoever and whatever. We care nothing for what they think, what they believe, what they plan, or what they dream. If they can pay our fee, we will fight and we will win, and then if *their* enemies want to pay our fee, we will fight for *them* and we will win! We are soldiers, we live well, and that is all that matters."

Sorel was up on his feet, pacing the platform. Degrange and the young black watched him but said nothing. He paced, looking sideways at the old maquis, Chantal, and Carter at the table below.

"I have heard about the skill of Nick Carter, the Killmaster, and now I have seen some of it. Skill and training and intelligence. We could use such a man, would give him the power and the authority he deserves, and would pay him the rewards he should have." He nodded to Carter, then turned his eagle eyes on Chantal. "We can use Mademoiselle Borotra's training and connections too. We can give her much more reward and position than France ever gave her or ever will."

"The reward you gave Captain Baudou?" Chantal said. "The position you gave him?"

Degrange and the young black officer looked at Chantal and at Sorel.

"I told you it was a waste of time, Commandant," Degrange said.

"You can't trust their kind anyway, General," the young black officer said.

Sorel waved his arms angrily. "Baudou was an idiot! He worked with us for three years and never saw what we were really doing. Then he decided to be a hero when there was nothing he could have done!" The slender commandant turned on Chantal. "Is that what you want? To live and die for nothing? A pawn in power struggles that benefit only the buyers and the sellers and the gang in power who serve them instead of the fools who voted for them? Die to defeat an enemy who will be a friend tomorrow? Die to protect what the rulers will decide to give away? Spend your whole life serving fat, arrogant men who do not even know your name and would not care about you if they did? Pieces in someone else's game to be swept away at will?"

Le Basque said, "You did not always speak that way, Sorel. When we fought the Nazis you did not speak that way."

"I was an idiot when we fought the Nazis! We were all idiots, dupes, fools! Has the world become better? Has France become nobler? Have people turned into angels or even honest men? Has genocide stopped? Forty years ago they were devils, inhuman demons. Today we forgive them! People say it all never really happened! We gave our blood, our friends, our families, our youth, and who has won in the end? The Nazis! It is not nobility and love and brotherhood that rule in this world, it is the children of the Nazis!"

The gaunt old man stood on the raised platform like some prehistoric bird in his anger. Half-crouched, he only slowly straightened up, his voice growing softer.

"Join us. We live and fight for ourselves. Not for hate or false loyalty, but for ourselves. For money, which has no hate or falseness, and our own lives."

"And us, Sorel?" Le Basque said. "Your old comrades who are too old to be mercenaries? What of us?"

Sorel smiled. "I am not so sure you are too old, Etienne. Or Daniel there. But if you feel too old for the field, we will take care of you. Completely. There is much work to do behind the lines. Your experience cannot be duplicated."

"I'm not sure I want to spend the rest of my life hiding underground, Commandant Sorel. And die a long way from France."

Sorel nodded. "We have installations outside the mountain, of course. A normal town. No one knows what is inside the mountain, eh?"

On the platform the white-haired mercenary leader watched the seven of them in turn. Degrange and the young black sat impassive. Outside the room, from beyond the corridors carved out of the solid rock of the mountain, the faint sounds of the soldiers in training reached the briefing room.

"And if we say no, Julien?" Le Basque asked.

Sorel shrugged. "It would be necessary to execute all

of you. Our existence is unknown, perhaps a vague rumor, and we must, of course, keep it that way. Still, if you join us, there is risk too. A soldier cannot be surprised at death. You will die, I will die, the difference is only how well we live while we wait.''

The gaunt, imperious old maquis strode back and forth on the raised platform, gesticulating, his eyes excited, his voice powerful, eager. ''With us you will live well, on the edge, eh? Excitement, pride, taking whatever you want, not bowing and scraping for the leavings the fat rulers toss you. Soon we will embark on the biggest campaign of my career! The most important job we've ever had. A hiring that will make us a fortune and will shake the world to its foundations. It will change the balance and end the rule of the new Nazis forever. So dangerous and difficult that no one but the Black Mamba Brigade could do it. Ten thousand of the best soldiers the world has ever seen. And we will do it! We will amaze the whole world! You can be part of it! Join us!''

His ringing voice echoed through the room. Degrange and the young black officer's eyes seemed to glow with the excitement that had poured out of Sorel. Carter jumped up.

''I'll join you! I'm tired of working for nothing, unknown, alone.''

Le Basque stared at the Killmaster. ''Carter?''

''Ah?'' Sorel said.

At the table on the platform, Degrange sat up. ''Commandant, I don't trust this American! He has tried to contact his superiors the whole time we have had him.''

''Of course he has. He is a first-class agent,'' Sorel said. ''Would we want a second-class associate?''

"But—" the younger black officer began.

"But he has *not* contacted his superiors, Major Christophe," Sorel said, "and he has not escaped, despite all his skills. We have taken his tools away with his clothes. We will test him. Without his clothes, what can he do? Even the Killmaster cannot claw through a mile of solid granite with his bare hands."

"He can kill with his bare hands," the black officer, Christophe, said.

"Then we must watch him," Sorel said. "But I don't think he will kill any of us if he agrees to join us. Not if the beautiful Chantal Borotra and her father also join us."

"Why not?" Chantal said. "It sounds exciting, and being shot is not exciting."

Le Basque looked behind him. "Daniel? Karl-Heinz? Everyone?"

The four old maquis from Paris looked at each other, then nodded. Le Basque shrugged.

"So, we all join. What do we have to do?"

"That you will be told later," Sorel said, beaming. "First there will be a long period of training and indoctrination. We will have you psychologically examined, tested. We must be sure. Eventually you will all take operational places—separately, of course, at least for a few years. Carter and Chantal will work with me personally. There will be assignments. But"—the white-haired commandant smiled—"we have certain methods of insuring your loyalty, which you will see."

"Must we stay in these clothes?" Carter said.

"Of course not. You will all go to the quartermaster and draw a proper uniform, a pay book, and be assigned quarters. I will talk to each of you later. Degrange?"

Sorel's scarred chief lieutenant got up. "Okay, then, all of you come with me. We will go to the quartermaster."

"Our, ah, weapons? Clothes?" Carter asked.

Degrange smiled. "You will not need those old things again, American. You are now in the Black Mamba Brigade. You will have new clothes, new weapons. Come."

Degrange led them out and along the stone passages with an escort of his gray-uniformed old maquis. The quartermaster storeroom was out of the command section and along another side corridor off the high-domed training area. Each of them were given uniforms. They dressed under the eyes of the old maquis, even Chantal. Degrange watched her. They were old, the resistance veterans, but they weren't dead.

"I cannot believe you really—" Le Basque whispered as he and Carter dressed together.

"There are scissors on that counter to cut off our tags," Carter whispered, smiling at Degrange and the other old men as they watched Chantal dress. The woman kept them very busy. "Get a pair, and when I turn my back do what I say."

Le Basque got the scissors and cut at his tags. Carter stepped in front of him. "The long scar inside my left thigh—cut it open and remove the cylinder. Now!"

"Cut—?"

"Do it, dammit, before Degrange comes over!"

Le Basque jabbed into Carter's thigh. Carter only smiled toward Degrange. Le Basque heard the faint click of the scissors hitting metal. He cut as Carter's teeth ground faintly against the pain, then removed the long thin alloy cylinder.

Carter took it and whispered, "Now, when we're

dressed, each of you knock out one of those old comrades of yours on my signal."

Le Basque nodded and finished dressing. He walked to Daniel, Karl-Heinz, Chantal, and the other two, talking casually as they all finished dressing. Carter stepped to the counter, smiled at the clerk who had handed out their uniforms, and held out his hand.

"I think I'm going to like the Black Mamba Brigade. Thanks for the help."

The clerk blinked, but shook Carter's hand. The Killmaster turned and said, "Now!" and stepped to Degrange.

Le Basque, Daniel, Chantal, and the other three jumped the old guards and knocked them out.

"Don't be stupid! There's a hundred men—" Degrange began.

Carter pressed the silver cylinder to Degrange's throat. "Look at the clerk! Nerve poison in this hypodermic. One sound from anyone and you're dead in two seconds."

Degrange stared at the body of the clerk sprawled across his counter. Dead without a sound. Without a movement.

"We're going out of here," Carter said. "Just you and us with Le Basque's people in your guards' uniforms. Those young soldiers won't know one old maquis from another. You'll take us out. Otherwise you're dead in two seconds, maybe less. How loyal to the commandant are you, Degrange?"

Degrange felt the tiny needle against his neck and looked at them all with hate in his eyes.

SIXTEEN

Degrange shrugged. "As the commandant says, it's living well that counts. I won't try to stop you."

"You always were a practical man, Degrange," Le Basque said drily.

"Why not? Why die for nothing? There is no way out of here."

"If there's a way in," Carter said, "there's always a way out." He turned to Le Basque's men. "Tie up all those old guards and put them into the back of the storeroom. Then everyone except Chantal, Le Basque, and myself dress in their uniforms. Fast!"

While the old maquis tied up their former comrades and put on their uniforms, Chantal watched the passage outside the quartermaster's supply room. No one came. Dressed, the four Parisian maquis came out with the AK-47s of the trussed-up Zaïrean maquis.

"Two in front and two behind," Carter instructed. "By now Sorel will have told everyone that we've agreed to join up, but they'll understand we're on probation. So guard us, but make it look casual. Chantal and Le

Basque will lead, and I'll walk in the middle with Degrange. Remember, Degrange, one word, one lifted eyebrow, and you'll be dead in two seconds or less.''

Degrange looked at the dead clerk still lying across the counter where he had fallen seconds after Carter's hand touched his. Sorel's old lieutenant nodded.

"Let's go," the Killmaster said. "Slow and easy. Chantal, Le Basque, look friendly, interested in the training, excited."

They went out into the stone passage and turned toward the enormous cavern where the soldiers were still going through their training exercises. No one passed them, and they emerged into the vast domed interior cavern. Some of the soldiers looked at them curiously, some smiled, some frowned, but none of them seemed surprised, as Carter had said they wouldn't.

"Smile," Carter said to Degrange.

Degrange smiled.

"Talk."

"About what?"

"Anything. Just talk. Tell me about the weather in Paris. Your glorious days in the resistance."

"Glorious? Not so glorious, Killmaster. Profitable, and useful, maybe, but not glorious."

"Keep talking."

They walked on around the perimeter of the cavern, skirting the training areas, with Chantal and Le Basque pointing out various interesting aspects of the training exercises. The soldiers and instructors watched them, but they barely glanced at the white-haired, balding guards.

"Where is the exit passage?" Carter said and smiled.

"Follow the rail tracks. The wide tunnel on the other side of the exercise area," Degrange said.

They passed the live ammunition combat course. The younger black officer, Major Christophe, seemed to be inspecting the operation, and he glanced up as they went by. He stopped and stared at them.

"Make it look very good," Carter said.

Degrange began to point out special aspects of the training and some of the installations inside the vast cavern. The exit tunnel was no more than twenty yards ahead now. Christophe watched them, watched Degrange, frowned, seemed puzzled, but he did not look at the old maquis guards. Carter nodded to the major, then asked Degrange a question. Christophe watched them a moment longer, then turned back to his supervision of the combat training.

"Nice job," Carter said.

"Merde," Degrange said.

Ahead, the narrow railroad tracks led into the wide opening of the passage out of the great cavern. A pair of armed soldiers sat at the entrance, bored, but obviously there on guard.

"Is there another way into that exit tunnel?"

"No."

"You have an explanation for why we're being taken in there?"

Degrange smiled. Carter touched his neck with the tiny hypodermic at the end of the long silver-alloy cylinder. "If we get captured, you won't know it."

"I'm taking you down to show you how secure the main gate is," Degrange said sullenly. "It's too far to walk; we'll take one of the cars."

The two guards came alert, saw Degrange, saluted, and relaxed a hair while acting as if they were still alert, efficient.

"Crank up one of the cars," Degrange ordered. "I'm

taking the new recruits to check out the gates. In case they're worried or get ideas, eh?''

The two soldiers grinned and pushed a jeep with wheels adapted for running on rails up to the mouth of the wide passage. Carter, Le Basque, and the four maquis helped lift it onto the rails. They all climbed in, and Degrange drove the jeep into the darkness of the wide tunnel.

Small lights illuminated almost a mile of smooth, blank stone walls without a break, until they stopped abruptly at a great black steel double door across the whole tunnel.

''It's a blast door,'' Chantal said. ''I have seen one in your Cheyenne Mountain complex of NORAD.''

''Yes,'' Carter said. ''The Black Mamba Brigade is prepared. How do we open it, Degrange?''

Degrange laughed now. ''You don't, Carter. I told you. They're H-bomb proof. They can't be opened except on the voice command of two top officers of the Brigade. Not even Sorel can open them alone. There's no way out, just as I said. You might as well give up and let me take you back.''

''If it can be locked, it can be unlocked. What's that door over there?''

A small, normal-sized steel door was set into the rock wall a few feet inside the gates.

''The control room.''

''Hold him right here, Le Basque,'' Carter said. ''Come on, Chantal.''

Together they opened the small door and went inside. The gate mechanism was ranged along one wall. Carter examined it closely.

''It's probably designed to fail-lock, so I can't destroy the mechanism or it'll lock even tighter. But there has to be a manual override for when the power fails. If we can just—"

"Over there. What's that door, Nick?"

Another door was set into the far wall of the small control room, a thick door with a pull handle and no visible lock. Carter went back into the tunnel.

"Bring him in here."

Le Basque brought Degrange into the control room.

"What's that door?"

"I don't know."

Carter touched the deadly needle to the old maquis's neck.

"Emergency exit."

"So?" Carter smiled.

"It's a foot thick, Carter," Degrange said. "Hardened steel. Even I don't know how it's opened."

"I do," Carter said.

He crouched at the heavy steel door. The lock was embedded deep inside, with only a small, round hole for a key: an electronic combination key, opening only on the meshing of electronic signals. Still, all locks had to have an actual mechanical unit to do the locking, no matter how it was activated.

"Everyone stand back."

Carter unscrewed the other end of the silver-alloy cylinder, drew out a needle-thin gray rod, and inserted it into the lock hole. He scratched the end, jumped back, and pushed everyone to the far side of the control room.

"Cover your eyes!"

There was a faint hiss, and then the small hole in the door began to glow with a dazzling light that grew brighter and brighter and everyone turned away. An acrid odor filled the air. The dazzling glow seemed to light up the room like the sun itself, an impossible glare that reflected off the walls, the ceiling.

"My God, the heat!" Chantal cried.

"Move aside!" Carter cried.

Chantal jumped out of the direct line of the door where the dazzling glow was slowly fading and then was gone. Carter turned and looked. The small hole in the door was a little larger now, but nothing more. Degrange laughed.

"Even you can't crawl through that hole, Carter!"

"I won't have to, Degrange."

The Killmaster went to the door, touched the handle, and easily swung the door open.

They all hurried through, and Carter pulled the heavy door closed behind them.

"With any luck, they won't notice any change in the lock," Carter said. "Or not for a long time, anyway."

A metal spiral stairway led upward, and they began to climb. The stairs went up and up and up until it seemed as if they would never end. Twice more there were other heavy steel doors, and Carter had to use his thin super-thermite rods. Then they reached the top.

"Wait," Carter said.

They were on a small steel platform, and another door was ahead of them. A light came from under the door. It was a much thinner door with a conventional spring lock that opened from inside. Carter opened the door slowly. The light came from an opening some ten yards ahead at the far end of a passage that had walls of dirt and brush.

A figure sat just inside the round opening at the far end of the tunnel passage. Carter motioned them all back, then he slipped out and along the dirt tunnel. The

gray-uniformed guard never heard him, and he collapsed unconscious instantly at the touch of Carter's
pressure on his neck.

Carter moved the unconscious man out of the way
and tied him up with his own belt. He motioned, and
they all stepped carefully out into the African sunlight.

"Sorel doesn't miss much." Carter said. "I'll bet that
exit has never been used or discovered, but he still had it
guarded."

"The commandant survives because he does not miss
anything, Killmaster," Le Basque said.

Dry, dusty, forested mountains towered all around
them. Below they saw a broad valley with houses and
streets and large factorylike buildings behind a high wire
fence. Inside the fence there were broad avenues among
the factory buildings, one at least a mile long and
straight as an arrow.

With Carter and Le Basque leading, Chantal bringing
up the rear with Degrange, they went down the mountain toward the town in the valley below. As they
reached the lower slopes, Carter looked for the entrance
into the secret mountain headquarters of the Black
Mamba Brigade.

"I don't see any entrance," Le Basque said.

"No," Chantal said.

Carter looked at the mountain, up at the sun, and
then at the town and large complex of buildings inside
the high electrified wire fence. Signs proclaimed
Katanga Metal Fabrique et Cie. Smoke came from the
stacks of some of the buildings. A large three-story
brick building with two flagpoles set in a lawn in front
of it was directly up against the mountain. The green
and yellow circle flag with the torch of Zaïre flew from
the left flagpole, the black, yellow, and red vertical

tricolor of Belgium flew from the right flagpole. The headquarters building of the metal company.

"That building is the entrance," Carter said. "It has to be. Clever and elaborate. There's no building and no metal company. It's the outside installation of the Black Mamba Brigade. No wonder no one has found them yet."

"A mercenary mountain, eh?" Le Basque said.

"Does anyone know where we are?"

"I do," Chantal said. "It's a town called Limbaba, in the mountains of Katanga. The Limbaba Metal Refinery of Katanga Metal Fabrique et Cie. If we go east, away from the sun up there, we should eventually come to Kolwezi, and find a Zaïrean army unit."

"Then that's our best bet. Head east for Kolwezi."

"That's across the valley and up that first ridge," Le Basque said. "We'd better stick to the mountains, away from the roads. They're bound to discover our escape soon."

"Agreed," Carter nodded. "We'll head directly east across the mountains."

"Nick!" Chantal cried.

The gray soldiers were pouring across the open spaces among the buildings inside the electrified fence. It was impossible to see where they were coming from. They were just there and spreading out.

"They've discovered our escape! Come on!"

They turned and ran across the slopes toward the mountains to the east away from the town and the "metal company" in the valley below. They moved quickly, covering the ground at a trained speed, until they reached the high point of the ridge across the valley from the bogus metal refining installation that hid the complex of the Black Mamba Brigade.

Chantal looked around suddenly. "Where's De-grange! He's gone!"

Carter nodded. "He slipped away when we ran."

"He'll tell Sorel where we're going!" Chantal said.

They crouched and looked back and saw the tiny figure of Julien Sorel, and then the gray soldiers all gathering around Sorel and a distant sticklike man that was Degrange. They watched Degrange point directly toward the ridge where they crouched.

"He's told them!" Le Basque said.

"I know," Carter said. "I wanted him to."

They all stared at the Killmaster.

"I want them to come this way," he smiled. "Because we have to go back."

SEVENTEEN

"Or," Carter said, "*I* have to go back. The rest of you can escape by going west deeper into the mountains until they give up. A small group with your experience shouldn't have any trouble evading."

"You'll go back into that mountain alone?" Le Basque said. "Why, Killmaster?"

"It's my job," Carter said. "I have to find out what the big attack Sorel is planning is all about. What, when, and where. Stop it if I can."

"That is my job too," Chantal said. "With you, Nick, or alone. But two will have a better chance of succeeding than one. Of getting the information out."

Carter nodded. "You're right."

"Then three should be even better," Le Basque said, and turned to his four old comrades. "Daniel? Karl-Heinz? All of you?"

The four old maquis looked at each other.

"I am not sure, Etienne," Daniel said. "We are a little old for this."

"Let us talk," Karl-Heinz said.

The four men moved away and squatted down in the thick mountain brush. Below, the gray-uniformed mercenary brigade was falling in behind the barbed wire, getting instructions from Sorel and Degrange and the other officers.

"How many do you estimate?" Le Basque asked.

"Two thousand," Carter said. "No more. The rest must still be in the mountain or off on some other assignments."

"Or in posts among these mountains," Chantal said. "Sorel would probably have outposts all through the area."

The four old maquis stood up and walked slowly to Carter, Chantal, and Le Basque. Daniel nodded to the west.

"We will try to escape. We are too old for real fighting. You will do much better without us, and if you do not, we are sorry, but we are too old."

Le Basque watched the four men. "Is that all, Daniel? You will escape, run to the west, because you are too old?"

"That is all," Karl-Heinz said.

"It could not be that you think to draw the enemy away, eh?" Le Basque said. "You think if you draw the enemy to the west, we will have a better chance of succeeding to the east?"

"We are too old for fighting," one of the other two maquis said. "That is all. We wish you success, but if we are to escape, we must go now."

"You will take the weapons," Le Basque said.

"It is you who will need weapons," Karl-Heinz said.

"No," Carter said. "Le Basque is right. Assault rifles won't help us, but they will you."

"Very well," Karl-Heinz said. "You are probably right."

"Perhaps," Daniel said, "they will follow us a long way."

"Maybe they will," Carter said, nodding.

The four old men picked up the Soviet Kalishnikovs, nodded to Le Basque and Chantal, and turned west. The three watched until they vanished over a spur and around the shoulder of the next mountain. Below, the gray soldiers were moving out in columns through the gates in the electrified fence, starting to wind up the slopes like long snakes.

"They will draw them west," Le Basque said. "A good chase if I know Daniel and Karl-Heinz."

"That will make our job a lot easier," Carter said.

"Follow them first?" Le Basque said.

"Follow them first," Carter said.

Chantal nodded, and they started up the slope in the footsteps of the four old maquis. They went a half mile up the ridge and over the crest to the downgrade before the rise of the first mountain itself. Le Basque spotted where the four old maquis had crossed a clearing of hard rock.

"Here?"

"As good as anywhere," Carter said.

Chantal turned left away from the trail of the old maquis and crossed the rocky area carefully. Carter and Le Basque followed, stepping lightly to leave no trail at all on the rock. They moved carefully along the rocky outcroppings, large boulders, gravelly slopes, until they found a dry stream bed. They moved on down the stream bed until it began to gather water and emerged into a running creek.

"Upstream," Carter said.

They turned and made their way back upstream as the creek narrowed and grew shallower and finally vanished into the ridge itself. Carter looked at his watch, then up at the sun still above the ridge to the west.

"They should be getting to where we watched about now."

"Just about," Le Basque agreed. "We'd better go to ground."

Chantal surveyed the trees and ridge above them. "Just under the crest would be best."

"There!" Le Basque pointed.

A large tree had fallen just below the crest of the ridge, its thick roots gouging out a deep hollow hidden by the torn roots themselves. The three agents climbed up along the line of the dry stream and the tree, and disappeared into the dirt hole behind the tangled roots.

"We'll need some weapons eventually," Le Basque said.

Chantal shook her head in the recess. "We couldn't shoot, not if we want to get back into that mountain without anyone knowing."

"We don't need weapons," Carter said.

"You always need a weapon," Le Basque said. "Every advantage you can get. Weapons can be silent."

They heard the first twig crack. A stone rolled down the slope of the ridge. Underbrush breaking, heavy footsteps.

Two thousand soldiers can't be silent.

A crashing through the bushes, heavy boots slipping on the slope, tramping as they tried to move forward quietly, searching the forest and the valleys for the escaped enemies.

Curses.

Laughter.

Boots on the trunk of the fallen tree.

On both sides.

Moving on and away down the slope of the ridge. There were shouts somewhere far off as other columns followed the trail of the actual escapees.

Silence.

In the dark recess, neither Carter, Chantal, nor Le Basque moved. They lay facedown as close to the edge of light from outside as they could get without being in the light itself.

And waited.

The footsteps were soft this time. Quiet. The crack of two twigs, a third. A pebble rolling down through the leaves. The steps of a single man beside the fallen tree.

A pale face peered into the dark recess under the roots.

Carter clapped a hand over the startled mouth, pulled the head, neck, and shoulders into the dark, and snapped the neck.

He left the feet outside in the light.

"Anton? Are you there?" a voice called softly in German.

"Over here!" Le Basque answered in German, his words muffled. "Come here! Quickly!"

Another pale face appeared on the other side of the fallen tree.

Chantal broke his windpipe with a single blow, clamped his neck between her shoulder and forearm, and strangled him.

The three waited in silence.

"There're always three," Carter said, and he slid out of the recess into the open, crawled along the fallen tree trunk, and peered over.

The soldier stood no more than five feet away, black, rifle alert, puzzled eyes looking toward where one pair of feet stuck out of the tangled roots of the fallen tree. Wary. Suspicious. Rifle raised to fire the signal.

He waited three seconds too long.

Carter was over the trunk and on the black mercenary before the soldier's head could even turn all the way to see what was about to kill him. He died, his neck broken, soundless on the forest floor.

Back in the darkness behind the roots, Carter checked the Kalishnikov and the knife. Le Basque had his, and Chantal held hers.

"That should be it," Carter said. "First the main line, then the three-man follow-ups in case we were smart enough to go to ground or climb a tree."

"There'll be a full rear guard back in the valley," Chantal said, "probably at the foot of the ridge or along the main road."

"And the usual security at the fence of the installation," Le Basque said. "But they'll be looking for these three sooner or later, and they'll know we are still here."

"Come on," Carter rasped.

They went out.

"Take a body."

They dragged the bodies down the slope all the way to the bottom of the ridge where the stream deepened and turned along the valley between ridges. They floated the bodies with their rifles slung over them, but they kept the knives. They watched as the three dead soldiers floated, bumped, and slowly moved along with the small current.

"Now it'll look as if they were killed and we went on to the west," Carter said.

They went back up the same slope past the fallen tree, because that was an area already searched by the dead men. Over the ridge the town below was oddly quiet, as if no one really lived there, as if it were all camouflage for the mercenary installation. They could see sentries at the gates of the supposed metal plant, and soldiers patrolling the road in the distance at both ends of the valley, but there were no gray soldiers between the high wire fence and the woods at the base of the ridge.

"At the base of the ridge," Carter said.

"Along the western edge of the road," Le Basque said.

"We can work north or south and outflank them," Chantal said. "Those sentries on the road have to mark the end of their line."

"Too much risk," Carter said.

"We could run into patrols, outposts, flank guards," Le Basque said. "Too many unknowns, girl. Better to head straight into their rear line and slip through."

They went down silently to within fifty yards of where the rear-guard gray soldiers lay hidden among the trees at the edge of the main paved road. Hidden, alert, invisible, but there was no enemy near, so small calls, laughter, cigarettes. When the enemy came they would be ready, hidden, but the enemy was far away, running from their comrades, so what was there to worry about? To be hidden from?

Carter, Chantal, and Le Basque lay fifty yards in front of the whispering, moving, restless line of waiting soldiers, and waited in turn. But they waited for night. For darkness.

It came, as it does in Africa, suddenly. The sun went behind the looming purple of the mercenary mountain, there was a glowing halo, and then blackness. Lights went on down in the valley beyond where the soldiers talked a little louder against the dark and smoked their cigarettes. A long line of glowing points of red visible for miles. All armies were the same, good and bad, when no enemy was near.

Le Basque moved first.

"I will go straight through between the large tree and the bush twisted like a hunchback."

He was between Carter and Chantal, and then he was gone.

They heard nothing. They waited five minutes.

"To the right, that wide gap between cigarettes because of the large boulder," Chantal said.

Gone.

Carter went silently behind her, moving like a shadow to the line of cigarettes, points of light like angry fire-flies. Down and crawled. Inched to within ten feet of the smoking soldier to the left. Through to the edge of the silvery road in the darkness, the first streetlights of the town two hundred yards to the left.

There was a touch on his foot, then Carter saw Chantal's face in the night.

"Your father?"

"Not yet."

"Here," Le Basque said.

They moved off in the direction of the main gate through the high fence. Trucks began to come along the road, then turn in through the gate. The guards opened the gate, waved them inside, and called for news.

"They've got 'em dug in two mountains over!" the drivers shouted.

"It won't be long now!"

"Keep the gates open!"

The guards did not inspect the trucks. Why would

they? Escape was the problem, not breaking in. Carter, Le Basque, and Chantal moved back along the road out of sight of the gate.

"We need uniforms," Carter said.

Chantal and Le Basque disappeared into the night. Carter slipped along the rear of the line of waiting soldiers, listening, watching. A point of glowing red showed where a single soldier sat against a tree behind the others. Carter crawled. His stolen knife entered beneath the rib cage without a sound; only a little blood stained the uniform he stripped off the dead man.

Dressed in the gray uniform, he waited at the edge of the road again. Le Basque wore a major's gray uniform. Chantal's slim uniform almost fitted, and she had tucked her long hair completely into her beret.

"I found a small one," the dark-haired woman said.

They all had automatic rifles and stood waiting for a single truck. One came, and Le Basque jumped out in front and waved it down, smiling at the driver, chattering in French.

"We need an empty! How are you?"

"Empty, Major," the driver said, leaning out the cab window. He was alone.

Chantal knifed him from the other side. Carter carried him to the rear of the covered truck, and the two of them hoisted the body up and climbed into the rear, where they stripped the body. Le Basque changed into the driver's uniform, and they drove to the gate.

"What's happening?" the gate guard yelled.

"Surrounded out there!" Le Basque called back as he roared through the gate. "Not long!"

Inside, Le Basque drove the truck along the broad, straight streets, waved on by military police.

"The buildings, Nick!" Chantal said in the dark of

the truck. "Jets inside! They're hangars!"

"And the long, straight roads are runways," Carter said. "They can probably move from here to almost anywhere in the world in hours."

"But where to this time . . . ?" Chantal wondered.

The MPs waved the truck to the right and then right again, and ahead the side of the three-story building against the mountain was wide open. Le Basque drove in and was waved left again.

"It's only a shell," Carter said.

"We're going inside the mountain," Chantal breathed.

The truck drove straight into the wide tunnel mouth and along the tunnel with its lights on until it came out into a long cavern full of trucks and tanks and personnel carriers.

"It's a different cavern," Carter noted.

"Their motor pool," Chantal said.

A last MP waved the truck toward the rear of the stone cavern that had a lower ceiling than the training area, and Le Basque stopped at the end of a precise line of parked trucks. The drivers were all leaving, chatting as they walked toward doors in the wall.

Le Basque jumped out of his truck. He waved to some of the other drivers. They waved back. Ten thousand is too many men for anyone to know everyone. Some of the drivers were no younger than Le Basque. Carter and Chantal slipped out of the back, fell in with Le Basque and some of the other drivers, and walked on through the doors into narrow passages. No one paid any particular attention to them. Inside their mountain they were so safe they had no suspicions.

The passage opened once more into the high-domed cavern they had seen earlier, and as Carter, Chantal, and Le Basque came out into the vast space, hordes of gray soldiers poured out of the main tunnel and began to fill the cavern, rank after rank. The three agents blended quickly in among the drivers who watched from the side.

Julien Sorel appeared riding one of the jeeps on rails. In the back of the jeep were Daniel, Karl-Heinz, and the other two old maquis from Paris. Their clothes were bloody, and their hands were tied behind them.

EIGHTEEN

Sorel stood on the hood of the jeep and shouted out over the ranks of gray mercenaries.

"What do we do with them?"

"KILL THEM!" the ranks shouted back.

"But they fought for their country!"

"THE FOOLS!"

"Who do we fight for?"

"OURSELVES!"

"I didn't hear you!"

"*OURSELVES!*" the ranks of gray soldiers roared.

The gaunt, hawk-faced commandant smiled. Commanding, imperious, with his white hair and slim, immaculate gray battle uniform, polished jump boots, blue beret. Fierce-eyed on the jeep above his soldiers, a leader on the battlefield, he stood tall.

"A second chance?"

"NO ONE GETS A SECOND CHANCE!"

"They were heroes."

"YOU WIN SOME, YOU LOSE SOME!"

"They have medals, honors, the gratitude of a grateful nation."

"MERDE!"

"What do we fight for?"

"MONEY!"

"Let me hear you!"

"MONEY!"

"Again!"

"MONEY!"

Sorel turned to face the four old maquis who sat in the jeep, bloody and trussed.

"You hear, old men? What do you have to say for yourselves? Tell my men here why you should be allowed to live. Tell them what use you are to them. They are practical men. What can you do for them, eh? Perhaps tell us where the other three are?"

Daniel spoke through broken teeth. "You did not speak like that when you fought for France, Commandant Sorel."

"Everyone has a right to be a fool once, old man."

Karl-Heinz shook his bloody head. "You did not think such filth then. *You* are the old man, Sorel."

Sorel's imperious face darkened. "I was as much a fool as anyone, yes. At first. A patriot, a lover of humanity. A bleeding heart and a democrat." The white-haired, eagle-eyed mercenary leader laughed. "But I learned—oh, how I learned! The Germans taught me much, but it was the French, the English, and in the end the Americans who taught me most! How I laughed at the end of that farce war when the Americans rushed so frantically to save Klaus Barbie, Mengele, and the other Nazi butchers—to help them all escape so they could use them against the Russians! How I watched while the

French patriots shut their eyes and turned their heads away while the Americans saved all those ever-so-useful murderers of the French people!''

He fixed the four old maquis with his intense eyes, then turned to the ranks of his mercenaries, his voice rising to reach the entire vast cavern. ''I learned things in the resistance, oh, yes! I learned that in this universe each animal thinks of nothing but itself. I saw human beings as they really are, and I came to despise them and the world they live in. Fools or murderers or hypocrites all! Nothing mattered, human beings are all animals, and it was then that I learned a man must work, fight, live, die only for himself! To fight for anything but yourself is idiocy. That was what fighting in the underground taught Julien Sorel! The great patriot, the marvelous maquis leader! So all the time I worked for the Nazis! Yes, the Nazis! That was how I survived so well! How we all survived!'' Sorel laughed violently. ''I worked for the Nazis, the Russians, the Americans, the English, anyone and everyone who would pay me and use what I could do—and they all admired me for it! I was useful, eh? I survived, I got rich, I came here and now I am richer, and I have the best killing instrument in the world. I live and fight and die for one thing. We all live and die and fight for one thing. What do we live and fight and die for?''

The ranks of gray soldiers roared out in the hollow cavern:

''OURSELVES!''

''MONEY!''

''OURSELVES!''

''MONEY!''

On the hood of the jeep Sorel waved them on, conducting the roaring voices. Degrange stood beside the jeep waving his arms. Major Christophe leaned in the wide tunnel mouth and watched. The Zaïrean maquis stood with Degrange and shouted with all the rest.

Sorel turned back to the four captured maquis.

"Do you hear them? What can you do for me, for them, that will convince us not to shoot you? Even old men want to live. What value are you to us?"

Daniel said, "We do not know where Le Basque, Chantal, and the American are."

"They separated from us after the first mountain," Karl-Heinz added.

Sorel snorted. "We know that. We found three of our men killed. Le Basque is a trained man—he would have arranged a place for you all to rendezvous. Where?"

"In Paris, Commandant Sorel. At the Arc de Triomphe," Daniel said.

"At the trial of Klaus Barbie, Commandant," Karl-Heinz said.

Sorel waved his arms angrily. "Take them to the wall!"

Chantal gripped Carter's arm in the last rank of the drivers. No one looked at them; all stared at their gaunt leader and the four prisoners.

"Will he?" Carter whispered to Le Basque.

"I don't know," the old maquis said.

Major Christophe nodded to a squad of twelve soldiers who stood apart behind the jeep as if waiting. They were of all nationalities, all races. From the medals on their chests, the campaign stripes on their sleeves, all were veterans of many wars and mercenary raids. They pulled the four old maquis from the jeep and marched them, stumbling, across the vast chamber, the ranks of mercenaries parting like the waves of the sea as they marched through.

"Papa?" Chantal whispered.

The squad marched the four maquis to a smooth area of the stone wall where six iron posts were set into the ground. They tied each of the old men to a post. The officer of the squad, an impassive Oriental with the insignia of Pol Pot's Khmer Rouge on his gray uniform, offered blindfolds. Each of the old men shook his head.

"We can't let them—!" Carter growled, staring over the ranks of gray soldiers to the four old fighters.

"You have a mission, Killmaster."

The officer offered each of the four a cigarette. They all took one. The officer lit each cigarette, stepped back, and marched away to the side. The old men smoked. Sorel stood on the hood of the jeep, his arms folded. Daniel was the first to finish his cigarette, and he flicked the butt away with his tongue.

Sorel looked at the four men tied to the posts. "Listen to me, old comrades. Tell me where Carter, Le Basque, and the woman were to meet you. Then join us, and you will be welcomed as full members of the Black Mamba Brigade. Refuse, and you will be shot."

Daniel nodded. "I believe you, Sorel. Your humanity has become a business deal. To welcome as a comrade, or to kill, has equal value. Such humanity I do not want."

"You are right." Karl-Heinz said, and spat away his still-smoking cigarette. "You are now no more than any animal. You and all your mercenaries."

The other two finished their cigarettes and spat them out. Every eye in the room was on the four men at the posts. No one made a sound. All stared toward the condemned men. Le Basque held Carter's arm and Chantal's. "We can do nothing. They knew what they did, Killmaster. We all know."

The Oriental officer snapped to attention.

"Ready!"

The squad raised their automatic rifles.

Chantal turned away. Carter's face was pale. There was nothing they could do. Nothing. They had to somehow stop Sorel and his Black Mamba Brigade.

"Fire!"

The volley echoed through the giant cavern, bounced back and forth from the rock walls.

The officer marched to each slumped body, shot each once in the head, then returned his pistol to its holster. He called his squad to attention, marched the squad through the parted ranks of mercenaries to Sorel, and saluted. Sorel returned the salute and dismissed the men to their places in the ranks of soldiers now at full attention before their commander.

"The other three will be found by our units still in the field, or they will escape to tell of us. It is of no importance!" Sorel shouted over the rows of gray-uniformed men. "They cannot harm us now. There is no time."

The ranks moved angrily, murmuring.

"What is important is our mission. The biggest mission of our existence. The impossible attack. For us it will be possible!"

Eager, excited movement rippled through the packed mercenaries.

"No one else could do it. No one else could be paid what we will be paid. This will be the single most highly paid mercenary raid in history. Each of us will retire rich!"

A surge almost like a cheer rose up through the disciplined ranks. A surge not of money but of blood.

"It is possible that we will, with one sweep, start World War Three and the end of this false civilization.

The beginning of a new civilization or nothing. A new world, or a cinder!''

Now the cheers were loud, real, the gray-uniformed mercenaries roaring, shouting.

"We will start it, and then we will come back here and wait. We will be ready for whoever wins, or if no one wins"—Sorel smiled—"or if no war begins, if it is allowed to pass, we will all be rich in this civilization. A fair gamble. We win no matter what happens."

Laughter in the ranks of the soldiers.

"Our task is simple: we will attack the city of Riyadh in the Kingdom of Saudi Arabia. We will destroy the air force on the ground, capture the royal palace, eliminate the king and all his ministers and advisers. We will eliminate as many of the royal family as is possible. We will hold Riyadh against all counterattack long enough for the Ayatollah of Iran to invade in full force and, with the aid of Saudi Islamic fanatics, of course, secure the country."

A sound like a low, animal growl filled the vast cavern as if the soldiers smelled blood, action, triumph.

"We will do this because we are the best, and because we"—the commanding leader stopped, fixing them all with his piercing eyes—"we have tactical nuclear weapons supplied by the USSR!"

There was an amazed silence, then a great wild roar of triumph as the soldiers cheered their leader. In the rear rank, Chantal and Le Basque looked at Carter.

"The Soviet czars do not wish to help us or the Iranians, but they cannot resist the chance to destroy an American ally, to secure influence in the area. No more than the Americans could resist destroying a Soviet ally and gaining influence in the Soviet playground. We will use these nuclear weapons. Then we will return, not to here in case the three agents do escape, but to another of our secret bases, and there we will watch to see if the world will plunge into full war, or if once more the fat men in power in both spheres will agree to continue their little game of musical chairs with the world, and the fools on the streets will let them.''

Laughter.

''The final triumph. We demonstrate our skill, feel the excitement of our work, and then live rich in this sick and ridiculous world of today, see the new world born in which we will have our part, or see everything destroyed, oblivion, and that would be our final triumph! To take the world, perhaps the universe, into oblivion with us! To destroy existence!''

Sorel's ringing voice echoed from the stone walls, and the ranks of gray soldiers cheered and roared until the sound was one great wall of violence. Sorel finally raised his arms in a great vee, then spread his hands out flat for silence. The room was silent.

''We mount up in two hours! To battle!''

The slender, ramrod-straight old man jumped down from the jeep and strode off toward the command rooms behind the rows of windows in the rock wall along the side of the room. Degrange fell in step behind him, followed by Major Christophe.

A gray-uniformed officer, blood on his shirt and violence in his eyes, came out of the main entrance tunnel and hurried across to where Sorel stopped to wait for him.

Among the drivers along the side wall of the vast cavern, Carter, Chantal and Le Basque watched the bloody, dirty officer talk earnestly, his arms waving. Sorel's eyes flashed even across the distance, and his face grew grim. He seemed to look all around the great stone cavern, and then he strode back to the jeep and jumped up onto the hood with the vigor of a man half his age.

Carter whispered to Chantal without looking at her or moving his lips: "They've found the ones we killed at the road."

Chantal and Le Basque nodded, then stared ahead with the other drivers as Sorel raised his arms again for silence.

"Three of our comrades have been found dead in the rear line! This means that the three agents who escaped did not continue west with the other four, but came back east."

Anger rippled through the stone cavern inside the mountain. Degrange climbed up with Sorel.

"They could have done this as a ruse, and escaped to the east," the renegade old maquis shouted, "or they could have come back to continue their action against us! To learn our plans and defeat us!"

The soldiers began to look around at their comrades. Among the drivers, Carter, Chantal, and Le Basque turned right and left to glare suspiciously at their neighbors.

"Let's find them!" Le Basque shouted in French.

"YES!" a hundred voices took up.

"FIND THEM!" a thousand voices responded.

Sorel motioned for silence. "I believe those old fools died to protect them, and they may even be somewhere inside the mountain now!"

Major Christophe climbed onto the jeep. "All commanders take their full squads and search every passage! Remember, one of them is a woman!"

Carter waved angrily among the drivers. "We'll search the passages on this side. Come on, five of you!"

Chantal, Le Basque, and three other drivers followed the Killmaster into the passage that led back to the motor pool cavern. Other drivers spread out, and the combat squads saw what they were doing and passed those passages by. Halfway to the motor pool, a side passage intersected, and Carter turned into it with Chantal and Le Basque behind him.

"We'll search this passage! You three search—"

Chantal stumbled, and her hat fell off. Her thick, dark hair cascaded down to her shoulders. For a split second everyone froze. Then Chantal pushed Le Basque to the floor and ran straight at Carter, her stolen combat knife aimed at his throat.

"You won't take me alive!"

Carter caught her wrist, saw her dark eyes fixed on him, and threw her to the ground.

"We've got one of them!" the Killmaster shouted.

Le Basque was up. "Take her to the commandant!"

Carter and Le Basque hustled Chantal down the passage toward the main cavern, shouting as they went.

"Here's one!"

"We've got one!"

"Here she is!"

The other drivers took up the cry, and soldiers poured into the passage from the main cavern. Carter and Le Basque slipped back and away and into the side passage they had been about to investigate.

Alone, they ran along the narrow stone passage, found a door, and slipped inside. It was a small round room, empty and dimly lit. The two men breathed hard.

"What will they do with her?" Le Basque asked.

"I don't know, *mon ami*."

The old man was pale. "She knew what to do. What she had to do."

"There was no other way. She knew it was her or all of us."

"No other way."

They stood in the darkness and listened to the soldiers moving along the passages. No one came past the door.

"They think this passage was searched," Le Basque said.

The sounds of the search suddenly grew less and finally stopped. A silence flowed through all the passages near where Carter and Le Basque hid. The Killmaster looked around the tiny room. In the dim light a flight of spiral stairs wound upward.

Outside the room there was no sound at all now.

"Up," Carter said.

The two men climbed quickly and came out in a long, narrow room carved from the stone. A tiny window overlooked the whole cavern below. All the gray-uniformed soldiers were in solid ranks. Sorel was in his jeep. Degrange and Christophe held Chantal between them.

Sorel's voice came muffled as if from a long distance, echoing in the enormous chamber below.

"We have one of them. The other two are probably in here too. For them I have a message! Killmaster—Etienne, old comrade—you can do nothing! We must leave now. We have no more time to look for you. We will hold the woman. If you try to stop us, she will die." The white-haired mercenary leader laughed. "You cannot stop us anyway. We will leave this mountain for you. Enjoy it. You will never leave!"

As Carter and Le Basque watched, the gray troops began to march quickly out. Far off they heard the sound of engines moving away.

NINETEEN

Nick Carter watched the last gray-uniformed soldier march into the wide mouth of the exit tunnel far below.

"No more motors," Le Basque said, listening in the dim room high above the cavern floor. "Nuclear weapons? Will they start World War Three, Killmaster?"

"Not if I can do anything about it." Carter turned to the spiral stairs. "Come on."

They went down to the small circular room and out into the silent passage. In the main passage they turned right to the motor pool cavern, which was as empty and echoing as an abandoned dirigible hangar.

They retraced their steps to the great main cavern. No one and nothing moved over the vast training floor. In the command section all the electronic equipment had been moved out. They walked through silent corridors, looking into empty rooms. In the quartermaster supply they found flashlights, and racks of Uzi submachine guns left behind, and ammunition. They each took an Uzi and as much ammunition as they could carry, and left their AK-47s.

There was nothing to shoot at now, but it made them both feel better.

In the rear of the quartermaster section they found all their own clothes and equipment neatly placed in wire baskets and labeled. Carter gathered up his weapons and devices, and returned them to their places. Le Basque retrieved only his beret and smiled as he put it on.

"Now I am ready to fight the devil!"

Back in the great cavern they hurried to the exit tunnel. There were no vehicles. Suddenly, all the lights went out. They stood in the pitch-darkness, no lights in the great cavern or anywhere along the black tunnel.

"Nick?" Le Basque said. "Listen."

Carter heard it. Silence. Total. Complete.

"No power, no blowers, no air coming in."

"How long?"

"It's a big installation. It'll be a few days at least before the air gives out."

They plunged into the tunnel and began to trot toward the distant blast door. They did not use their flashlights; they might need them more at some future time.

In the tunnel itself the air seemed heavier, harder to breathe, and Le Basque had to slow to a walk sometimes as they moved through the thick darkness. After a time they lost any sense of space or time in the dark world without dimension. They could have been on some unknown planet, in an unknown time.

The sense of something looming up ahead rose up like some great monster of the earth.

Carter put out his hand.

Touched.

Smooth, cold, hard.

"The blast door," Carter said. He switched on his flashlight.

They hurried into the control room and across to the emergency exit door Carter had melted open on their earlier escape. It lay inside the circular stairwell. Blasted. The two men stood and shined their flashlights upward.

The emergency exit had been destroyed, the stairs gone as far up as they could see.

"The commandant is thorough," Le Basque muttered.

Carter searched above for any way he could use his escape wire, but there was nothing within range to catch it on; the stairs were destroyed all the way up to the first sealed door.

"Very thorough," Carter said.

"Your thermite? Will it work on the blast doors themselves?"

In the dark tunnel again, Carter examined where the two halves of the blast door joined. The juncture was all but invisible. There was no lock opening. At the bottom the gates moved on rails, but they were so tight to the floor, a separation did not exist. Designed to be radiationproof, there was no space to insert the thin thermite rods.

"All I can do is tape a rod to the face of the door and hope it burns through to the lock. Not confined, the thermite doesn't work that well, and I only have three left."

"Then it can't be done," Le Basque said.

"No," Carter said.

They stood in the dark tunnel. Only Carter's flashlight dispelled the blackness, and the air seemed thin and heavy at the same time. Oppressive, stifling, forcing their lungs to labor, gasp. They knew the air could not give out so soon or so quickly, but the whole weight of the mountain seemed to press down on them, crush them.

"The control room." Carter said.

While Le Basque shined his flashlight, Carter examined the control mechanism again.

"Fail-locked, that's how the door was designed. When they cut the power, the doors remained locked automatically."

"That means they cut the power from outside."

Carter nodded. "They'd have their own power inside, but they probably inactivated that first, then cut from outside. Everything would be fail-locked, but that means there must be a manual override."

"That would only operate from inside," Le Basque said.

"Inside, and locked up, and only top officers with a key. Find it!"

They both searched the control room, each starting at one side and working toward the center. It was Le Basque who found it.

"Here, Killmaster!"

It was a large solid square cabinet of hardened steel at the base of the main computer locking mechanism and had the same kind of round-hole lock for an electronic key. Carter took one of his last three thermite rods from the silver-alloy cylinder and inserted it into the lock hole.

"Get back," the Killmaster said.

He stood across the room with Le Basque, eyes averted, as the glow once more filled the room, the pungent odor spread, and the wave of heat. The glow brightened to a dazzling brilliance and slowly faded away leaving only the heat in the small room.

The two men returned quickly to the heavy steel cabinet and together swung open the door to expose a large wheel and another small, locked box.

"The override switch," Le Basque said.

Carter took his next-to-last thermite rod, inserted it

into the lock hole, and scratched.

The brilliant light again filled the small room as the two men turned away.

Soon, in the darkness and the heat, they bent over the small box and opened it.

"There it is," Carter said, nodding to Le Basque. "Go!"

The old maquis unslung his Uzi and went out into the dark tunnel.

Carter threw the simple electronic switch and began to turn the large wheel. In the darkness, the wheel turned easily, a smooth gear reduction mechanism working with soundless precision. He turned until the wheel would turn no farther.

There was no sound from out in the tunnel.

Carter held his Uzi and went out. Le Basque stood smiling. The heavy blast doors were open. Far off he could see a faint glow of light.

No guards had been left outside the gate.

It was Julien Sorel's first mistake.

The Killmaster and the old resistance fighter lay in the thick bushes at the base of the mountain. The sky was nearly as black as the inside of the tunnel, but the night glowed brilliantly under hundreds of floodlights as the Black Mamba Brigade prepared for its biggest attack.

All the "factory" buildings were open now. Hundreds of gray-uniformed mercenaries worked around mammoth jet transports, some American and some Soviet, built it was impossible to know where. Giant, jet-powered attack helicopters were being rolled out onto the long runways, the bright runway lights making long paths into the darkness.

The top floor of the tower of the fake industrial administration building was lit up, with air controllers on duty. Just below the top of the tower, Sorel, Degrange and other command officers stood on an open balcony watching the preparations and relaying orders through computer terminals inside the command room behind them.

A loudspeaker boomed out, *"All commanders, D minus one hour. Repeat, D minus one hour."*

Across the open spaces behind the electrified wire fence, and outside in the supposed town, the gray-uniformed mercenaries gathered their weapons, gear, supplies, parachutes, bulletproof vests, and all the other special equipment of an elite assault shock force. Ten thousand crack troops.

"Can they do it, Nick?" Le Basque asked.

"They can do it," Carter said. "Ten thousand well-trained assault troops could take and hold just about any city on earth for a few days. With tactical atomic weapons"—Carter shrugged—"maybe for a long time —if they didn't start World War Three in the mean-time."

"No one is that insane."

"Don't bet on it," Carter said. "The Ayatollah is nuts for sure, and I wouldn't bet on their Chairman or our President if the fear or craziness got big enough—if it gets to look like one of our systems is definitely going to lose."

"Then we must stop Sorel before he leaves the ground!"

"If we even try, they'll kill Chantal."

Le Basque suddenly looked older in the night, with only the eerie illumination of the distant floodlights to outline the hollows and shadows of his face behind the thick bushes.

"Sorel must be stopped, Killmaster. No matter what."

Carter nodded. "Maybe we can do both. At least we can try."

"One can always try," the old maquis said, staring out into the illuminated night. "The runways, Killmaster—we must destroy the runways!"

"Or the nuclear weapons."

"Both."

Carter watched the preparations among the brightly lighted buildings and the open fields. "We've got an hour—probably an hour and a half if I know army units—before they're ready. Sorel's mistake in being so sure we couldn't get out of the mountain means our escape isn't likely to be discovered. We have an hour to contact Hawk and locate Chantal."

"Then let us do that," Le Basque said.

In the gray field uniforms of drivers of the Black Mamba Brigade, the two men moved through the night among the shadows at the edge of the floodlights. Soldiers walked quickly, ran, crouched, sat, and lay catching the last few minutes of sleep before battle. They were everywhere across the grass and dirt, around the hangars and jets, under the helicopters. No one noticed two more soldiers hurrying to some urgent destination with their Uzis ready.

They found the small command helicopter standing alone behind one of the hangars.

"You! Halt!"

The single guard stared at them as they started to climb into the helicopter.

"What the hell do you think you're . . . Hey, you two are those—"

Le Basque hurled his flashlight into the solitary sentry's face. Carter smashed his Uzi against the man's head. Le Basque caught his throat as he staggered. The sentry went limp. They dragged the body into the helicopter and climbed in. Carter found the radio.

Le Basque watched at the helicopter door.

Carter located the secret AXE wavelength, then gave the special call numbers that would connect him to the AXE computer.

"Hello, N3, you've been a bad boy. The director is furious."

"Dammit, this is urgent! Top secret, Director Only. I want—"

Hawk's anxious voice came on the line. "What's going on, N3? It's been days—"

Carter cut him off. "We are on the base of Black Mamba, sir, under attack. We have only minutes." In rapid-fire sentences he tried to give his boss as many details of what was happening in the briefest possible time. He felt like a tape recorder on fast forward.

"Ten thousand? Trained?" Hawk's voice was almost a whisper. "Nuclear weapons from Russia? Can this—"

"The attack will succeed!" Carter interrupted again. "They must be stopped here."

"Two hours. One and a half at best. That's all I can promise. The Sixth Fleet is two hours' flying time away. Hold them for two hours, N3."

"I don't know, sir," Carter said quietly. "We can try."

"Try, Nick."

Two hours. And the Black Mamba Brigade would be ready for takeoff in less than forty-five minutes.

TWENTY

"Where would Sorel hold Chantal?"

Le Basque thought. "Close to him, yes, but not where she could hear what is happening. He used to say to me, 'Etienne, you never know when someone will escape, no matter how impossible.' So, not where she could know what was going on, but where it would be the most difficult to rescue her."

Carter shook his head. "The buildings are all hollow —façades and hangars—except for that tower on the administration building. She has to be in there."

The old maquis looked across the floodlit runways from the bushes inside the fence where they had buried the dead sentry. The guard would be missed before the attack took off, but he wouldn't be found. Not before. A deserter.

"We can't take the risk, Nick. If we try, we could be killed, captured, immobilized. The attack would go off before your planes could arrive. They might or they might not catch them and stop them. No, we have perhaps half an hour before they go, an hour to hold them here. We have no choice."

Carter nodded slowly, staring across the night toward the tower and the distant figures of Sorel and his officers. In the wide floodlit space between, the whole complex was alive with the gray soldiers preparing for their mission.

"There may be one chance—the nuclear weapons," Carter said slowly. "If we can find them—use them— we could destroy the runways and maybe the planes themselves, and hold the Mambas here until the fleet jets arrive. Then, while the navy attacks and keeps Sorel and his killers busy, we could save Chantal."

"*If* we can find the weapons."

"They have to load them in the transports."

"But we don't know what weapons they are, what they look like."

"I do," Carter said. "Field pieces and recoilless shoulder cannon. Some bazookalike weapon for breaching walls. They're Soviets, and I doubt if Sorel would bother to repaint them. They're dark gray with red markings."

"The transports or the helicopters?"

"Let's find out."

They crawled silently away from the fence to the edge of the glare of floodlights behind the first bogus industrial building. Inside, the ground crews were working on two fast jet transports, testing and loading at the same time. There was nothing Carter could identify as the tactical nuclear weapons.

All across the open fields between the buildings the gray-uniformed mercenaries were forming up in their units, falling in, preparing to board the transports and helicopters.

The loudspeaker boomed out over the whole installation in the garish night: "*D minus thirty minutes. First transports load in ten minutes. D minus thirty min-utes.''*

Carter and Le Basque circled the building at the edge of the light. At the side of the large hangar they saw a stack of medical boxes, red-cross armbands, supplies. Carter took two armbands, giving one to Le Basque and putting the other on. They picked up a large box marked with a red cross, and walked boldly out into the glare of light and across the open space to the next hangar.

The forming ranks of the mercenaries paid no atten-tion to them. The one time when all armies are the least alert is when they are moving out for an attack. That's why there were MPs, walking in pairs through the buildings, among the tents, around the barracks. But the only MPs Carter could see this time, beyond those who were directing traffic along the roads and runways, were stationed around a concrete blockhouse behind the next building. Their military police jeep was parked and ready in front of the door.

''Le Basque!''

The old maquis saw the red-helmeted soldiers, their MP armbands clear on their immaculate gray fatigue uniforms, Uzis hanging around their necks, pistols at their sides. There were six of them, grimly alert, for-midable, yet rigid at parade rest, immobile as statues. It was a mistake some military minds make: the imposing façade instead of the flexible force.

''The nuclear weapons have to be in that bunker,'' Carter said.

The blockhouse was at the edge of the floodlights, three quarters in darkness, and none of the units were close. It was as if there were standing orders for all troops to stay far away. Another miliary error: isolation isn't safety.

"The two at the back can't see the two at the front," Le Basque said.

The loudspeaker boomed: "*D minus twenty-five minutes, first units to the loading areas. D minus twenty-five minutes.*"

The Killmaster and Le Basque drew their knives. Le Basque dropped to the ground and crawled toward the MP on the west side of the concrete blockhouse. Carter disappeared silently to the east side.

Carter struck first, rising up out of the dark ground like a ghost to bury Hugo under the ribs of the first MP. He whirled to the front before the dead man hit the ground, then hurled Hugo into the throat of the second startled MP, and broke the neck of the third. He saw Le Basque grappling with a fourth over the body of the fifth, then raced to the rear to cut the throat of the last as Le Basque plunged his knife home and ended it.

The two men breathed hard. Twelve seconds had passed. They did not waste time hiding the bodies.

The lock of the steel door on the concrete blockhouse opened to the last of Carter's thermite rods.

Inside, the dark-gray-and-red nuclear projectiles were lined up in careful racks: shells and rockets for recoilless cannon, bazookas, mortars, and large field pieces. Rows of the recoilless cannon, bazookas, and mortars were there too, as well as other ammunition.

"Those are chemical shells," Carter said.

"Gas?" Le Basque said. "*Mon dieu!*"

"Regular ammo too, but we want the nuclear stuff. Let's take a mortar, a recoilless cannon, and two bazookas, and all the shells we can carry."

"There! The carriers."

Le Basque picked up two of the heavy canvas carriers that hung like ponchos back and front with large pockets for the shells. He picked up two of the deadly gray-and-red projectiles.

Carter swore. "Damn!"

"What is wrong, Killmaster?"

"No krytrons!"

"Krytrons?"

"The tiny switches used to trigger nuclear weapons! Without them the shells are not fused. Look around!"

They searched, but the krytrons were not there.

"They must be somewhere!" Le Basque said.

"We don't have any more time. Someone will spot the bodies soon now. We'll have to try to hold this building."

Le Basque looked around. "Impossible, Killmaster. No windows, nowhere to fire from. We would have to dig in outside and they would run over us in minutes."

Carter nodded. "All right. Take all the conventional weapons we can, and some of the nuclear stuff. Maybe they won't know they're not armed. We'll load the jeep out front, then find a hole up on the slope of the mountain. With mortars and cannon we can cover the runways, and they'll have to blast us out before they can risk a takeoff."

"It would be suicide, Nick!"

"But maybe we'd live another forty-five minutes. That's all we need—just forty-five minutes."

Le Basque went out. Carter gathered up two mortars, two recoilless cannons, two aprons of shells, and two boxes of concussion grenades. He dragged them outside. The night was silent at the blockhouse, the dead MPs lying in their blood. Everywhere else the base was in frantic activity, troops marching, the transports being slowly wheeled out, ranks and ranks of gray soldiers already lined up along the runways.

*"D minus fifteen minutes. First transport is loaded.
Commanders for second transport commence loading.
D minus fifteen minutes."*

Together they loaded the weapons into the military
police jeep, then returned for more shells, and still
more.

"That's all it can carry," Carter said.

"Let's go! They will see us at any moment!"

"Blow up the blockhouse! Get rid of the nuclear
weapons!"

"Later, Killmaster," Le Basque said. "I am sorry."

Before Carter could turn, he felt the blow on his
head, the strong fingers on his neck, the pressure. . . .

The Killmaster came awake. Gunfire echoed through
the night. He touched where his head was bleeding.

Heavy gunfire.

Darkness.

He sat up. He was in some kind of hard ditch, behind
trees, beyond the light. There was blood on his hand,
but not much. His weapons were all in place; he had the
Uzi around his neck, a bazooka, and an apron of ammunition in the ditch beside him.

The heavy firing was not far away.

The floodlights were off! He could see only the small
lights outside the buildings, along the roads behind the
fence, and in the fields where he saw the ranks of gray
soldiers lying down looking toward the mountain. Flat
on the ground.

Carter crawled to the edge of the ditch and looked
over.

He was in a concrete-lined drainage ditch close to the
false administration building near the base of the mountain.

On the mountain, a hundred or more yards up, the military police jeep was on its side in front of two large boulders. Even as Carter watched, the jeep's heavy machine gun fired across its side from between the rocks. Four gray uniformed mercenaries fell seventy yards below on the steep slope.

Bodies of gray soldiers littered the slope.

More tried to move upward.

A concussion grenade lobbed over the rocks, exploding directly among them. The survivors dragged the fallen back down to the vehicles all along the base of the mountain. Behind the vehicles the gray soldiers crouched. Carter could see Sorel, Degrange, and Major Christophe, all staring up the hill at the improvised fort, shouting orders.

A mortar shell exploded among the vehicles, scattering soldiers in all directions.

Another mortar shell exploded on the main runway.

Le Basque!

The rocks, with the jeep on its side, formed a natural fort, with only the steep approach in front, and no way to get above it.

Carter looked at his watch. He had been out maybe five minutes, no more.

Forty minutes.

The mercenaries could not risk a takeoff on the main runway as long as Le Basque was there. Forty minutes. Could Le Basque hold out that long?

Already the gray soldiers were moving closer, using the rocks on the steep slope for cover. More and more were coming up.

The nuclear weapons?

No, Sorel would not use them on one man on a hill. Not until he had to. And he would not have to. Le

Basque was a dead man. The only question was when.

How long could he delay the mercenaries? How long could he hold out without help, without Carter getting into the battle?

There was no way on earth he could join the old maquis. Any attempt would only expose Le Basque. All he could do was open another attack, sabotage the transports, but the tough old man had not chosen to fight alone because he wanted all the glory.

Le Basque had hit him, put him out, so that he, Carter, could rescue Chantal while Basque created the diversion.

Carter could not let it all be for nothing.

TWENTY-ONE

Carrying the recoilless cannon, wearing the apron of ammunition, the Killmaster raced along the hidden drainage ditch. More mortar shells exploded behind him, tearing at the vehicles and runways.

The ditch ran behind the wing of the fake administration building, then vanished beneath where the building joined the mountain. The tower rose in the center, directly over where the wide tunnel went into the mountain inside the building.

A recoilless cannon shattered the night where Le Basque was making his stand, followed by the chattering of the machine gun and the *boom* of a grenade.

The sound of a helicopter!

Carter whirled to look up at the black sky. The chopper was rising slowly over a distant hangar.

The Killmaster turned back and smashed a window on the ground floor of the building, climbed in, and dropped to the floor of the cavernous hollow inside the building. To the left he saw the dark opening of the tunnel into the mountain.

No one was in the building.

Stairs on both sides of the wide tunnel entrance led up to the upper floors of the tower. The firing and explosions shook the whole building. The helicopter motor grew louder.

Carter ran up the stairs to the first floor of the tower. Two soldiers were seated in the central corridor, smoking and listening to the battle, relaxed, enjoying being out of the fighting. They jumped up when they saw him, guilty, afraid he was an officer.

"*Who is it*?" one exclaimed in German.

"*Where is she*?" Carter demanded, going on in rapid German. "The prisoner! The commandant wants her. Now! *Schnell!*"

"Next floor, sir! Second room. We . . ." The soldier stared. "You're not . . . you're that—!"

They both tried for their rifles too late. A single short burst of the Uzi slammed both back against the corridor walls, pitched them forward dead to the floor.

The Killmaster jumped over them, grabbed an AK-47, and took the next flight of stairs three at a time. The third-floor corridor was empty again. He could hear voices up on the top floor, the control tower, everyone up there watching the battle that reverberated down the stairs and from the walls.

The helicopter was closer, its rotors shaking the tower.

Carter kicked in the door of the second room. Chantal sat on the floor, her leg chained to the wall. Her dark eyes were wide, her hair down on the shoulders of the gray mercenary uniform. She stared at him as if she could not see him, as if she expected to see someone else, anyone else.

"The firing?" she said.

"Your father," Carter said, motioning her away from the wall.

She stood away. He severed the chain with a burst.

"Alone?"

Carter nodded. "There may still be time to help."

"The blood on your head?"

"His work. He made the diversion and left me to find you."

"The old bastard," she said tightly.

"Come on!"

He tossed her the AK-47. In the corridor they went up to the command floor. Deserted, the computers and terminals flashed, murmured electronically, computed without a human presence.

The violent explosion rocked the tower.

Two computer terminals toppled to the floor, smashed. A bank of computers went dark and silent.

Through the window, over the command balcony, Carter and Chantal saw the pieces of the helicopter falling in flames. Le Basque stood among his rocks, the bazooka still on his shoulder. Below him on the mountainside gray soldiers were running and stumbling back down the slope to the siege line of vehicles, many of the trucks and jeeps now shattered wrecks.

Angry voices raged and cursed up above. Two soldiers came down the stairs, sliding and stumbling, eager to do battle with someone.

They didn't see Carter and Chantal.

The Killmaster plunged Hugo. Chantal smashed with the butt of the AK-47. They dragged both bodies into a corner, then went up the stairs to the final floor, the control tower.

They were all at the windows staring at the smoldering remains of the helicopter. Recoilless cannon shells from Le Basque were exploding along the main runway and among the vehicles below his position on the mountainside.

Someone heard Carter and Chantal. Turned.

"Enemy! Down!"

Carter lobbed a grenade from the stairwell.

Another.

The explosions shattered the room, scattering blood and bone and pieces of arms and legs. Among the screams and moans, someone opened fire. Carter and Chantal raked the room with bursts from the stairwell.

The firing stopped, and the screams and moans faded.

The two agents climbed slowly up into the room, but they found no one alive. At the windows they looked out at where the gray troops were halfway up the slope toward Le Basque's redoubt. From the tower they could see the old maquis's head and shoulders where he fired the machine gun, bent to fire the mortar, swung the recoilless cannon to shoot another great hole in the main runway.

"Look!" Chantal cried.

Two more helicopters were approaching the mountainside. Carter ran back down the stairs to the command floor where he had left his recoilless cannon and shells, then raced back up. The helicopters were closing in; the gray soldiers were moving up closer now. No firing came from the redoubt.

Chantal had field glasses and stood watching her father in his stand on the mountainside.

Le Basque looked up at the two helicopters approaching inexorably, separated so that he could not get two quick shots at them.

It did not matter anyway.

He looked down at his feet. There was one more bazooka shell, and no cannon projectiles.

Two grenades, the machine gun ammunition gone.

His Uzi with two more clips.

He looked at his watch. Thirty minutes.

He smiled.

Thirty minutes was a long time to have held out.

He watched the helicopters approach.

He searched the whole installation below. He saw the gray soldiers moving up the slope, wary, cautious. He had not fired for five minutes, but he had hurt them badly, and they came on cautiously.

But it wasn't the helicopters or the soldiers he was thinking about. He searched the field for a sign of Chantal. Of Carter. The Killmaster and his daughter. He knew the American would have known what Le Basque had done and why.

Where was Chantal?

His old eyes searched, hoped.

The helicopters were poised to swoop in now, the gray soldiers no more than ten yards below the rocks. Le Basque took a deep breath, tossed his last two grenades over among the mercenaries, listened to them scream, and raised the bazooka with its last rocket.

A helicopter vanished in a roaring sheet of flame!

Le Basque looked left. The tower! The American stood at a window at the top, a recoilless cannon still on his shoulder. The Killmaster—and Chantal!

The old man saw the slim, dark-haired figure of his daughter, an AK-47 in one hand, binoculars aimed toward him in the other.

Chantal.

Le Basque laughed aloud, and fired the bazooka at

the remaining helicopter. Its rotor exploded, and it plunged into the side of the mountain like a wounded bird.

Then the old maquis jumped on a boulder, Uzi in hand, and waved wildly toward Chantal and the American, the gray mercenaries no more than five yards away down the slope.

He looked at his watch. Thirty-five minutes.

He smiled, and opened fire as the gray troops stood up and rushed toward him.

It was as good a way as any for an old fighter.

In the shattered control tower, Carter and Chantal watched the second helicopter fall into the mountain, then saw Le Basque jump on his boulder.

They saw him wave to them, laugh, and open fire with his Uzi on the swarm of gray soldiers rushing up the mountain.

They saw the mercenaries sweep over the jeep, the boulders, and the old maquis.

Chantal turned away.

"Thirty-five minutes," Carter said.

Chantal leaned against a blood-spattered wall, her head down, silent.

"He saw you," Carter said. "That's what mattered."

She breathed hard and squatted down, arms around her knees, head against her arms, dark hair hanging almost to the floor.

"Now," Carter said, "it's up to us. They'll be coming. We have to hold out five, ten minutes."

The woman was motionless. Then nodded, breathed, stood up, and turned to the smashed windows.

Below, the gray soldiers were converging in a mass on the tower. Sorel, Degrange, and Major Christophe rode in a jeep behind the first wave of running soldiers coming toward them.

Carter smiled. Sorel's second mistake. Carter and Chantal were no real problem now. They had no more big weapons to stop the transports. Le Basque had done a good job on the main runway, but the cross runways were usable, the transports could go out with lighter loads.

But Sorel was maddened by bloodlust; he thought of nothing but destroying the last resistance. And the mercenaries advanced on the tower.

"Save your ammo for when they reach the stairs," Carter said.

"How many shells do you have left?" Chantal said quietly.

"Two. And three grenades."

The dark-haired woman looked out toward where Sorel had ordered up two field pieces.

"Can you reach those two guns?"

"I can try."

Carter shouldered the long cannon. Chantal loaded it. Carter fired.

Across the distance the field gun seemed to leap into the air on a spout of concrete, dirt, and smoke. The second gun fired. The tower rocked, and glass and plaster showered around the two agents. A gaping hole appeared in the floor below.

Carter fired again.

Missed.

The dirt, concrete, and flame spouted up ten yards to the right of the gun.

"Take some grenades," Carter said.

Chantal nodded. They divided the grenades. A second shell smashed into the tower above them, took off half the roof, and knocked them both to their knees. They struggled up, and heard soldiers in the hollow space of the first floor far below. They took up positions where they had a clear field of fire down the stairs, a clear throw of their grenades.

"We've stopped them," Carter said. "There's no way now they can regroup and get off before the navy arrives."

"No," she agreed with a weak smile.

"Your father did it."

"We all did it. You, me, Daniel, Karl-Heinz—all of us and your agent Lyons too."

"What will Sorel do?" Carter wondered.

"Run, hide, try again. He's a fighter too, the commandant."

They heard the running, pounding feet almost up to the floor below. Carter took a deep breath and glanced out the window.

It was a speck at first. Then rapidly a dot. A shape. Three shapes. Six. In perfect formation.

Like a single unit the six U.S. Navy jets swept in low, dropped their bombs, cannonaded and machine-gunned, mowing down the gray uniformed mercenaries who stood and stared upward unbelieving.

The next wave swept in, and the next, and the next.

In minutes the Black Mamba Brigade was destroyed, its installation a shambles, the transports and hangars burning, the helicopters exploded, the runways and houses rubble.

All through the ruins the mercenaries dropped their weapons and fled.

Carter and Chantal went down the stairs warily. No one stopped them. At the bottom the empty space echoed hollowly to the gunfire and explosions outside as the jets swept in again and again. They turned toward the exit.

And Julien Sorel made his third mistake.

"Killmaster!"

Carter and Chantal whirled.

Sorel and Major Christophe had come out of the wide tunnel entrance into the mountain not twenty feet away and opened fire with their Kalishnikovs.

A bullet slammed Carter to the floor, shot his Uzi out of his hands. Chantal got off a single burst, cut down the young black major, then fell and lay motionless.

Sorel rushed forward firing as Carter rolled.

The imperious, commanding old man seemed to hang in midair for a moment, the stiletto sticking out of his throat. Then he collapsed with his blood pouring across the floor of the hollow building.

Holding his left arm, which hung bloody, Carter struggled to Chantal. She sat up, an ugly wound on her head. Ugly, but only a graze.

"I'll have a hell of a headache. You?"

"Some stitches, a sling."

They came together and held each other as outside the U.S. jets began to land on the destroyed base.

Hawk and the Zaïrean general stood on the slope of the mountain where Le Basque had died. Carter and Chantal, bandaged, Carter's arm in a sling, stood beside them.

"He held them thirty-five minutes," Carter said.

"You all did well," the Zaïrean general said. "My country is grateful."

Below, the Zaïrean troops who had come in after the

U.S. Navy were rounding up the last of the mercenaries.

"What happens to the Black Mamba Brigade now?" Chantal wondered.

The general shrugged. "They will scatter. Some we will capture, put on trial; others we won't. They'll find other mercenary units, fight for a hundred other causes and rulers. But as a unit they are destroyed."

"Because Sorel had to kill Carter," Hawk growled. "If he hadn't, he might have escaped to try again. He was the Black Mamba Brigade. Without him, it is over." The AXE chief shook his head. "How can men go so wrong? Start out with all the ideals and end in hate so deep they can destroy the world."

"Not all men, Monsieur Hawk," Chantal said. "My father died as he had lived—for his ideals."

Hawk nodded. "Perhaps there's some hope."

The AXE director and the Zaïrean general walked down the slope where the Zaïrean troops held the captured and bloody mercenaries, Degrange sullen among them.

Alone on the hill where Le Basque had died, Chantal and Carter looked out over what had once been a green, peaceful valley.

"Where to now?" Chantal smiled.

"The Riviera? A few days?"

"Why not? Without guards it might be fun."

They both laughed, and looked out over the shattered valley.

"There is hope, isn't there, Nick?" Chantal asked. "One man kept his hope for the world. If one can, perhaps all can someday."

Then they walked down the scarred mountain to the jet that waited to fly them out.

DON'T MISS THE NEXT NEW NICK CARTER SPY THRILLER

BLOOD ULTIMATUM

The frogmen surfaced from out of the Shark River by moonlight. Methodically, each one of the four pulled himself onto the rocky bluff called Comanche Point. One by one, their eyes lifted to the precipice where, nestled snug in the quiet village of Westport, lay Commonwealth Power's nuclear reactors 1, 2, and 3. The reactors' white domes stood stolid as though impenetrable as the four men in black wet suits plodded up the bank, each carrying the necessary supplies.

Once on top, they reconnoitered the monstrous complex and its surrounding 250 acres. The moon cast its wicked stare upon them. The river ran swiftly like an inky ribbon below as the leader of the group cut through the barbed-wire fence separating them from the reactor site. Each climbed through the wire barrier with caution, then stripped their wet suits for the lead-lined models designed for radioactive exposure.

The leader nodded to two of them. "It is time," he said decisively.

Weapons drawn, the group separated into two teams.

The first pair headed toward the center of the complex where the security headquarters was situated. The second left for Reactor 3, Comanche Point's newest and most powerful generator.

The three guards stationed at Central Security could not know what lay in store as the two armed men entered. One had time to rise from his chair, but he was greeted by a .45 hollow point. Tagged in the heart, he was sent reeling backward into a wall, his chest gushing blood. The others could not react, died clutching coffee cups as they dropped to the floor.

The first of the killers holstered his silenced weapon. The other stepped outside the bulletproof building, and his eyes combed the surrounding area vigilantly. Meanwhile, his comrade searched each of the three dead guards. His hand was wet with blood as he pulled a small plastic card from the captain's pocket. He ran his fingers over its embossed numeral.

"Yes," he whispered, pleased.

He placed it in a slot marked "Systems," then watched as the panel lit: *Corridors 1, 2, 3. Security Section II. Reactor 1. Reactor 2. Reactor 3.*

It was Reactor 3 that concerned him. In the final stages of refueling, it was most valuable. Moreover, their inside contact had left security gaps a mile wide.

The second team reached Reactor 3 without incident. The site was patrolled at regular intervals, so there was no room for slipups as the two men moved toward one of its three entrances. They separated as the guard left the office building to the left of the pressurized steam stack, and one of the team shot a silenced round that blew off the back of the guard's skull. The assailant stood hidden some twenty feet away awaiting reprisals as his accomplice tossed an egg-shaped gas grenade into the reactor's entranceway. The two seated guards reached for their throats. Their eyes bulged grotesquely as they fell face forward onto the desk, then made soft, choking noises as they succumbed to the deadly phosgene fumes.

There was a cautious silence. Again nothing.

The domed reactor, which could become a beehive of commotion, remained silent as a tomb. The men secured their gas masks. The leader patted down the guard for his security card, then entered it into the slot marked "Systems." The panel lit: Security Section II. Reactor 3. Corridors 1, 2, 3, 4. The leader pushed the button marked Corridor 1. The panel door slid open. He entered, a 50mm machine gun leveled chest high.

"Come," he said to the other, who held a suitcaselike vessel.

He followed as the first of the technicians appeared from the labyrinth of corridor doorways. A volley of silenced machine-gun fire turned the technician's laboratory coat red before he could say a word. Another followed. Then another. The sound-sensitive devices seemed deaf to the slaughter. The second assailant followed, tossing a gas grenade into Corridor 1, then into each of the technical labs along the way. The building was cylindrical with the reactor at its core. They walked toward the reactor room entrance. The heavy door was of reinforced steel. The concrete walls were four feet thick. The locks clicked open as the security card was introduced. Finally, the fourteen-inch-thick steel panel slid open. A round of fire followed, killing one of the two nuclear technicians.

"Don't move!" the armed man snarled.

The technician raised his hands in the air. "This is insane," he sputtered. "What—who—"

The leader slid on his belly under an electronic beam.

"Shut up, Mr. McClusky," he told him.

The leader dragged the containment vessel behind. He stood, then raised his .45 automatic. He eyed the petrified McClusky for a fraction of a second, then walked to the 950,000KW reactor. He stood over the spent fuel pit. "Raise the fuel rods," he ordered.

"You're crazy!" the technician rasped. "Those rods are highly radioactive! We'll all be contaminated!"

"Raise them!"

"I can't—I won't!" he said, sweat streaming down his face.

The leader calmly fired a bullet into McClusky's forehead.

"Come," said the leader in Spanish. "We must work fast."

The second man moved to the fuel pit, a virtual well where the energy-giving fuel rods were "cooled" for 120 days during refueling. The leader stepped up the metal staircase briskly. He neared the computer panelboard. His eyes blinked rapidly as he strained to remember its intricate code. He punched the first three digits. The number and letter combination lit on the keyboard. The second man made ready the containment vessel as a fourth, fifth, sixth, and seventh combination followed. The leader paused. He pulled the release lever slowly. The two men watched in awe as the tubular rods containing the fuel element U232 began their ascent from the depths of the water-filled pit. The stainless steel shroud rose with an electrical hum. The lift halted. The leader set the shroud's digital lock, and the head sprang open. The leader looked at his watch, then to the man who handed him a mechanical retrieving device. With precision, he lifted the five-inch-by-ten-inch rods, then placed them individually in the graphite and asbestos vessel. Suddenly, the lights flickered. The generator's monotone hum stopped. The lights remained in a brown-out state for a split second, then returned to normal.

"A detection device," the leader said in Spanish. "Radio *now*!"

The second man pulled a walkie-talkie from his side.

"Green 0215," he whispered, looking at his watch. "Repeat. Green 0215 hours."

The leader bolted the containment vessel and lifted it.

"Come, we must go."

They secured their gas masks, then passed under the electric eye, knowing detection would seal the reactor building in seconds. They passed through the huge panel door and back into Corridor 1. The phosgene fumes still rose like steam from the concrete floor. They walked briskly, the leader carrying the bulky containment vessel at his side. The radioactivity had reached outlandish proportions as they ran from the corridor and exited the reactor building. Ripping off their gasmasks, they cast their eyes skyward where a Huey helicopter hovered twenty-five feet above. The two ran toward the copter as it lowered itself to the ground.

Security headquarters had been ignited in a diversionary effort. The second team ran from the blazing building as security men emerged from the Reactor 1 and 2 areas. The four terrorists mowed them down mercilessly before shoving the containment vessel into the copter, which still hovered slightly above the ground.

"What happened? For Christ's sake, what happened?" one of the first team screamed.

The leader threw himself into the copter. Two others followed as the aircraft's churning blades stirred a blinding dust cloud. The last of them took a bullet and clutched at his side as the copter rose vertically. The leader returned the fire, killing the guard, then looked downward to his wounded compatriot.

"Lo siento," he whispered coolly, then fired two .45 slugs deep into the man's chest.

The chopper reeled away at a 45-degree angle, leaving a score of men dead or dying. Security headquarters blazed in the moonlight. A lone alarm echoed eerily behind. Comanche's Reactor 3 had been robbed of plutonium, the makings of an atomic bomb.

—From BLOOD ULTIMATUM
A New Nick Carter Spy Thriller
From Charter in April 1986